Marian Pearse

SPY-IN

Pete, Linc and Julie enroll for a semester of danger on a small college campus, as they try to find the men responsible for an athletic gambling fix.

The teen trio encounters much more than they signed up for including Mafia infiltration, militant agitation and murderous confrontation—in their scramble to find the mystery man behind the sinister syndicate. . . .

ANOTHER SMASHING MOD SQUAD ADVENTURE!

SEE THE EXPLOSIVE TV SERIES STARRING MICHAEL COLE, CLARENCE WILLIAMS III and PEGGY LIPTON

THE MOD SQUAD #4

RICHARD DEMING

The Mod Squad #4
SPY-IN

A PYRAMID BOOK

First printing August, 1969

Printed in the United States of America

PYRAMID BOOKS are published by Pyramid Publications, Inc.
444 Madison Avenue, New York, New York 10022, U.S.A.

CHAPTER 1

ALTHOUGH it was still a full week before the fall semester began at Baldwin Hills College, Athletic Director Mark Doyle had been putting in eight to ten hour days at his office for the past ten days. In addition to conferences with his various coaches, there was still some game scheduling to complete, some delicate string-pulling necessary to arrange the last-minute admission as freshmen of a couple of star athletes belatedly discovered in some backwoods village by the football coach, plus the hundred and one other things that always beset the athletic director of a sports-oriented college in the weeks before school starts.

Doyle's problems were complicated by his secretary having married and moved East during the summer. Administration hadn't yet gotten around to sending him another, with the result that he had to do all his own typing and clerical work. As he had only a rudimentary knowledge of filing procedures, it sometimes took him as long as a half hour to find some document he needed.

It was nearing 6 P.M. when Doyle locked the door to his private office. Before he could cross the outer office to the door leading into the hall, a slim, shapely brunette wearing trim tight white slacks and an equally tight white sweater came through it. She was an exceptionally pretty girl with finely chiseled features, a beautiful mouth and a milk-white complexion.

It was twenty years since Mark Doyle had been chosen an All-American end. In the interim his then almost constant interest in the opposite sex had ebbed to the point where his romantic life involved only his rather colorless wife of eighteen years. But he still noted and remembered the prettier faces and trimmer figures he spotted on campus. He didn't know this girl's name, but he knew she was a student because he had seen her crossing the quadrangle with an armload of books on a number of occasions. He even recalled that she had sometimes been accompanied by track star Scooter Miller.

The girl gave him a rather strained smile and said, "I phoned your home, Mr. Doyle, and your wife said you were here. Do you have a few minutes?"

"Well, how few?" he asked, thinking of the iced Manhattan his wife would have waiting in the freezer compartment of the refrigerator.

"I won't keep you long. It's about the bribes some of Baldwin Hills' athletes took to hold down scores last year."

Mark Doyle stared at her for several seconds, then turned and unlocked the door to his private office. He gestured the girl in ahead of him and carefully closed the door behind him. Pointing to a chair in front of his desk, he waited until the girl had seated herself, then rounded the desk and sank into its upholstered swivel chair. He didn't have to turn on the light because at that time of year—the last week in August—there was still sunshine at 6 P.M.

"Let's start by giving me your name," Doyle said.

The girl primly folded her hands on top of a leather bag she had laid in her lap. She gave her head a slow shake. "Let's start with an understanding. What I have to tell you is in strict confidence. I want your agreement in advance that I won't be called to testify in court or even before any school board of inquiry."

Doyle contemplated her broodingly for some time before saying, "I can't make any promises until I've heard what you have to say. Accepting bribes to throw athletic events is a criminal act, and I would be morally bound to have you subpoenaed as a witness if your words constituted the only evidence of such acts. If you can furnish me enough information to establish a case without your testimony, I am willing to agree to do everything possible to protect your anonymity."

After considering this, she nodded. "I'll accept that. My name is Eve Evans, and I'm a sophomore. Or rather I was last year. I'll be a junior when school starts."

The athletic director flipped open a note pad lying on his desk, took out a ball-point pen and wrote down the name. The girl frowned at this indication that what she had to say was going to be taken down, but she made no objection.

"Address?" Doyle asked.

"The girls' dorm. Or do you mean my San Francisco address?"

"I meant your local address," he said. He wrote down "Lowell Hall," then put the pen away and steepled his fingers. "How come you're here a week early? I didn't think the girls' dorm was even open yet."

"Oh, yes, except you have to get special permission, and they don't serve meals. Several girls are staying there."

Doyle for the moment tabled asking why she had returned to school a week early in order to get to more important matters. "Now what's this about our athletes accepting bribes?"

"I can only give you one name," Eve Evans said. "But I know that at least three track men besides him, plus some football players and a couple of basketball players were paid to goof up last year."

Doyle again examined her in silence for several seconds before speaking. "Admittedly we had a bad track season last year considering the talent available, but since we took the conference football championship and made a second place in basketball, I find that statement a little incredible, Miss Evans."

"I didn't say that the players threw games, Mr. Doyle. They only threw points. That's all the bookies who fix games care about. They don't care who wins or loses. They just want the point spread held to a safe figure."

After thinking this over, Doyle nodded understanding. "I don't bet on college events, but of course I'm aware that the odds-makers declare an official spot for contests, usually based on the majority opinion of the major sportswriters."

"That's right. And when you bet on a college game with a bookie, you have to accept the declared spot. Say, for instance, the sportswriters pick Baldwin Hills for a fourteen-to-nothing football victory over Chico

State. If you bet on Baldwin Hills, you don't win unless they score at least fifteen points more than Chico. All the bribed players have to do is make sure Baldwin Hills doesn't get ahead more than two touchdowns."

After considering again, Doyle said slowly, "The point spread would work for the overall score at a track meet, too. But not on individual events, and I imagine lots of people would want to bet on them. There's no way to spot a race. A sprinter can't win or lose the hundred-yard dash by so many points. He either wins it or loses it, period. So we had a bad track season."

"You're getting the point, Mr. Doyle."

"Yeah," he said dourly. "Who's the bribe-taker whose name you said you know?"

"Lloyd Miller."

Mark Doyle's eyebrows shot up. "Scooter? He was one of our few track men who had a pretty good year."

"All except for our February 14th meet with Ventura Junior College, the March 7th meet with Moorpark and the March 28th meet with Valley State. Look those up."

Doyle pulled his substantial frame erect and strode into the outer office. After fruitlessly searching through a number of file cabinet drawers, he slammed the last drawer shut in disgust and muttered something under his breath. He returned to the inner office and resumed his seat.

He said, "I can't find the records, Miss Evans. As a matter of fact, I can seldom find anything in those blasted files. My secretary quit and I don't have a new one yet. You'll have to refresh me about those meets."

"All right," the girl said agreeably. "Scooter was four-to-one favorite to take the hundred in all three meets. Two he lost convincingly enough, because the winners had pretty fair times. But he had to stumble to keep from winning in the Moorpark race. The winner plodded in at 10.1."

After thinking, Doyle nodded. "I remember that one. And I was feeling sorry for Scooter!" His brow furrowed in a frown. "How do you happen to know about this, Miss Evans?"

"Scooter told me. We used to go together."

"Used to?"

Her expression became disdainful. "He's decided he's in love with some frizzled blonde he met in summer school. He had to attend summer school to make up some courses he flunked, so that he can graduate next June. He isn't very bright, you know."

That seemed obvious, Doyle thought, or he wouldn't have confided his misdeeds to a girl he planned to drop.

He said, "Do you know who bribed Scooter to lose those races?"

"Just the man's name. It's Eddie Kye. K-Y-E. Who he is or what he does for a living, I couldn't say. I don't think Scooter really knows either. He had the man's phone number, but once he mentioned that he didn't even know where Kye lived. He used to phone him, then meet him in some tavern to pick up his money."

"Did you ever see this Eddie Kye?"

The girl shook her head. "I just know of him from what Scooter told me."

"Do you remember the phone number Scooter called?"

She shook her head again. "I never knew it. He just mentioned he had it, but he never said what it was."

"How about these other athletes you claim also accepted bribes?"

"I only know about them from what Scooter said, too. He never told me any names. But after the Moorpark meet he told me three track men aside from him had been paid to throw events. At other times he mentioned football and basketball games being fixed."

Mark Doyle studied her for some time in silence, trying to decide if she really knew the other names and was protecting all but Scooter Miller because her grudge was only against him. There was also the possibility that Scooter was innocent, of course, and that she had made up the whole story merely to get the boy who had jilted her in trouble.

Presently he said, "Were any sports other than track, football and basketball involved?"

After thinking this over, the girl said, "I really don't know. It seems likely that this Kye man would be interested in baseball and swimming and all the other competitive sports too, doesn't it, since they all could be bet on? But Scooter only mentioned the ones I told you about."

Doyle was again silent for some time. Finally he said, "You haven't given me any evidence other than your personal knowledge, Miss Evans. I don't see how I could agree not to involve you in the investigation that is bound to ensue from what you've told me, because you constitute the whole case."

She gave him a bright, brittle smile. "I'll make it easy for you to see a way, Mr. Doyle. I deliberately caught you alone, so that in case you decided to have me subpoenaed, I could deny ever talking to you. And I will, even under oath. I have no intention of testifying to what I've told you under any circumstances."

"Why?" he asked with a frown. "Do you care if Scooter learns that it was you who told on him?"

The girl rose to her feet and stood gripping her leather bag with both hands. "Not particularly, but I am concerned about the possible reaction of Eddie Kye and his associates. It occurred to me that some criminal organization might be behind these bribes—possibly even the Mafia. And I'm not too confident in the police's ability to protect witnesses against organizations like the Mafia. So I decided that my contribution to law and order would be merely to tip you off to the situation, and not to help you prove it. No arguments by you or anyone else will change my mind about that, so we may as well drop the subject. Okay?"

He gave a resigned shrug and stood up also. "If that's how you feel about it."

With another bright but meaningless smile, she turned to go. He stopped her at the door by saying, "Miss Evans."

Turning, she said, "Yes, sir?"

"Why are you at school a week early?"

"I had some business to attend to locally and decided it would be cheaper to live at the dorm than at a motel."

"This business involved Scooter Miller?"

Eve flushed. "Some of it."

"When did you discover he had another girl, Miss Evans?"

Her expression became haughty. "I consider that my personal business, Mr. Doyle."

"It became my business, too, the moment you walked in that door," Doyle said quietly. "It's quite obvious your motive in reporting this is revenge for Scooter jilting you. I have to consider the possibility that you made the whole thing up just to avenge yourself."

After staring at him for some moments, she said indignantly, "Well, I didn't." Several more moments of silence elapsed before she said, "If you have to know, Scooter wrote me toward the end of summer school that he was in love with this blonde tramp. I had a summer job and want it again next summer, so I couldn't just quit and come down here then. I got in town two days ago, and we had a face-to-face talk. He made it quite definite that we were through for good. Does that satisfy you?"

He nodded. "Thanks for coming in, Miss Evans."

"You're welcome," she said with sardonic bitterness and went out.

CHAPTER 2

NONE of the three walking along the corridor toward the office of Captain Adam Greer looked old enough to be a cop. And they certainly weren't dressed like cops. Yet all three were.

The tallest of the three was a lean, well-muscled black youth about six feet tall and weighing around 165 pounds. He had a handsome, rather serious face, even white teeth—the front ones spaced slightly apart—and wore an Afro haircut. The white youth in the group had the same general build but was about an inch shorter and five pounds lighter. He also was good-looking, with green eyes and light-brown, curling, unruly hair worn moderately long. The girl walking between them was a slim ash blonde with long straight hair that hung loose nearly to her waist. She was of average height, had brown eyes, delicate features and an exceptionally nice figure.

The two boys wore tight denim slacks, sneakers and open-necked sport shirts with the tails hanging out. The girl wore a bright red-and-yellow dress with a miniskirt, thong sandals exposing bare toes with red nails, and carried a straw handbag.

Although they might have passed as teen-agers, all three were beyond the statutory age limit of twenty-one required for membership on the Los Angeles Police Force. The trio comprised what had come to be known throughout the department as the Mod Squad.

The Mod Squad was the brain child of Captain Adam Greer, who had encountered considerable resistance to the suggestion when he first broached it to his chief. Greer had reasoned that a squad of apparent teen-agers would be more effective in certain undercover roles than older cops. Because he contemplated using them at least some of the time on juvenile assignments, he had wanted squad members who understood the problems of the young, particularly of youngsters who had run afoul of authority. The best place to recruit that type of youth, he figured, was from the ranks of juvenile delinquents. All three had once been in trouble with the law as juveniles, but had long since straightened out their lives.

Another unmentioned reason Captain Greer had in the back of his mind, when he was pestering Chief Metcalf to let him form the squad, was that he hoped working on the side of law and order would have the therapeutic effect of keeping the three former juvenile delinquents straightened out. He had never mentioned this reason to the chief, because Metcalf didn't believe in appointing cops to the force for what he called "social work reasons."

Despite having gone much the same rocky route as juveniles, the three members of the Mod Squad came from widely varied backgrounds. Lincoln Hayes, the black youth, had been one of eleven children in a ghetto family. Peter Cochrane, the white youth, was the only child of a wealthy Beverly Hills businessman and one of Beverly Hills' most prominent clubwomen. Julie Barnes, who had grown up in San Francisco, had no idea who her father was and seldom heard from her mother anymore, except when her mother needed money.

Julie Barnes said, "Didn't the captain even give a hint as to what he wanted to see us about?"

Linc Hayes said, "When did he ever?"

"He went so far as to intimate it was another undercover assignment," Pete Cochrane told them.

"Oh joy," Linc said. "Will we get to wear costumes, like on Halloween?"

"He didn't say. Maybe he'll put us in policeman suits and make us pretend to be cops."

The trio halted before the door lettered: CAPTAIN ADAM GREER. Pete Cochrane rapped.

After the captain's voice called, "Come in," Pete pushed the door open and let Julie and Linc precede him inside. He shut the door behind him.

Captain Greer, sitting behind his desk, was around forty. Squarely built, he had an intelligent but rather stern face. He wore a dark, well-pressed, conservative business suit.

The man, sitting in front of the desk, rose to his feet. He was several inches over six feet tall and looked as though he had once possessed a rangy build, but his waist had thickened with middle age. He had a pleasant, deeply tanned face and shaggy hair beginning to become quite gray on top.

Captain Greer introduced the visitor as Mark Doyle, Athletic Director of Baldwin Hills College in Los Angeles. He added the information that Mr. Doyle was there because he had received a tip that professional gamblers were bribing athletes at Baldwin Hills in order to control the scores of sports events.

"Sit down and I'll let Mr. Doyle give you the details firsthand," the captain said.

When everyone had found seats, Mark Doyle explained that his tip had come from a co-ed named Eve Evans, but that the girl absolutely refused to appear either in court or before a school board of inquiry.

"She's afraid of retaliation by the gamblers," Doyle said. "She's got it in her head that some sinister organization such as the Mafia is behind the bribes. Actually, it's probably just some local bookie. The briber's name is Eddie Kye."

Captain Greer said, "That doesn't ring any bells." He added, "At least with me," and glanced at the three members of the Mod Squad.

All three shook their heads. Linc said, "As it happens, most of the bookies in this town are controlled by the Mafia, Mr. Doyle. Maybe the girl's got a point."

Doyle looked faintly surprised. "There's Mafia control of crime in Los Angeles?"

"We do our best so suppress it," Adam Greer said dryly. "But there's some Mafia influence in every big city in the country. For the benefit of the Mod Squad, go over again just what Eve Evans told you."

Mark Doyle described in detail what the girl had reported to him. When he finished, he said, "Of course, I immediately contacted Dr. Vester, the college president, to report the incident. Dr. Vester decided the potential situation was too serious merely to have an investigation by school authorities. He instructed me to take no personal action whatever, but to turn the whole matter over to the police. I haven't even discussed the situation with my various coaches. Aside from you people, Eve Evans, Dr. Vester and I are the only ones who know there is anything to investigate."

When Doyle stopped talking, the three members of the Mod Squad simultaneously turned inquiring gazes at Captain Greer.

"Chief Metcalf decided it was a job for you guys," the captain said. "So he sent Mr. Doyle here. You boys are both going to be star athletes, transferring to Baldwin Hills as juniors from some small college back East."

"How about me?" Julie asked.

Mark Doyle said, "Captain Greer tells me you type and have done office work in the past."

Julie glanced at him and nodded.

"It just happens that my secretary resigned at the end of the last school year. Administration is supposed to be hiring me another, but they always drag their feet until school actually starts. I can easily arrange for you to be the replacement. That will give you access to all athletic records and will also put you into contact with all of the coaches and many of the athletes."

"All right," Julie agreed.

Pete said, "What sports are Linc and I supposed to star at? Neither of us are tall enough for basketball nor heavy enough for football."

"It will have to be track," Doyle said. "That's best, anyway, because you won't have to demonstrate your abilities. Usually our track coach doesn't even start his men on conditioning exercises until about the middle of October. So you'll only have to talk about your records, you won't have to prove them."

"We might be able to hold our own, anyway," Linc said. "I did some running in high school and also threw the javelin. And I've heard Pete mention being a jumper."

Doyle examined both with interest. "What kind of records did you have?"

Linc said, "I was strictly a second-place man. I ran the hundred in 9.8 and once threw the javelin two-hundred feet."

Pete said, "I was just a second-placer too. My record high jump was only six feet four, and my best long jump was twenty-three feet."

Captain Greer said, "You mean broad jump?"

Pete and Linc both grinned at him. Linc said, "You're dating yourself, Captain. It's been the long jump for some years."

Mark Doyle said, "Those records wouldn't bring any scouts to look you over, but they're fair enough for high school. Probably you'd improve in college, so we'll boost them a little. Let's say you now do the hundred in 9.6, Linc, and heave the javelin two-hundred-thirty feet. Pete, we'll let you do the high jump at six feet seven and go twenty-three and a half feet at the long jump."

Captain Greer asked curiously, "Why those precise figures?"

"Because they're good enough to compete in our league, but not so good that they would draw the attention of any syndicated sportswriters. If they were any better, the track coach, their fellow teammates and any gamblers who might try to bribe them would wonder why they never heard of Linc Hayes and Pete Cochrane. If they were any worse, nobody would have to bribe them to lose."

The captain nodded. "That makes sense. Now pick a college for them to transfer from."

"I already have," Doyle said. "My brother is a professor of music at a little school called Central College in Fayette, Missouri. I'll phone him tonight and have him airmail me the necessary blank transcript forms used by Central College. We can type in the pertinent information after they get here. I'll arrange to have all the necessary records appear in the proper files through Dr. Vester, so that if anyone goes to the trouble to check, the transfers from Central will appear legitimate. I'll also arrange for you two to room together in the boys' dorm."

"Will I live in the girls' dorm?" Julie asked.

The athletic director shook his head. "School employees usually live off campus. You can continue to live at home." He examined her brightly-colored dress and red toenails with admiration, but it was tinged with dubiousness. "School employees usually dress a bit more conservatively too, Julie."

She grinned at him, unoffended. "I won't embarrass you, Mr. Doyle. I have some plain skirts and blouses."

"Good," he said, grinning back. "Can you start work tomorrow?"

Julie looked surprised. "I thought school didn't begin until the day after Labor Day."

"It doesn't, but I can't find anything in my files."

Julie glanced at Captain Greer, who chuckled. "May as well give him a lift, Julie. Mr. Doyle was telling me earlier that he's having something of a clerical problem."

"All right," Julie agreed. She turned back to Doyle. "What time?"

"Nine. My office is in the Athletic Administration Building, which is right in front of the Field House."

"I'll be there," Julie said.

CHAPTER 3

WHEN the meeting in Captain Greer's office broke up, the three members of the Mod Squad headed for the Records and Identification Section on the second floor of the Police Building. Pete asked the girl on duty behind the R. and I. counter to see if there was a package on an Eddie Kye.

There was one under the name of Edgar H. Kye. There was no way to tell if this was the same man Eve Evans had reported as Scooter Miller's briber, but the trio went into the record room to pull his package and study it.

The record room was a huge room with shelves on three sides in the shape of a U. Every person within the jurisdiction of the LAPD who had a criminal record had his individual manila envelope stored here. These were stacked upright, like books, on the shelves, and the yellow color of the envelopes gave the shelves a golden cast. As a result, the unofficial name of the room was the Golden Horseshoe.

Packages could not be taken from the room, but in the area between the shelves there were tables at which police officers could sit to study them. Pete located the proper envelope, and the three of them sat at one of the tables to examine its contents, Julie in the middle.

Edgar H. Kye was listed as aged forty-two, unmarried and as having only a grammar-school education. He had a record of fourteen arrests over the past twenty years, most of them on minor gambling charges such as selling numbers tickets or chances on lotteries. Two were for assault, however, both complaints being later withdrawn. There was a note in the record that Kye at that time was believed to be a strong-arm collector for a loan-shark named Dinny Cord, and that both victims were believed to owe the loan-shark money. Apparently, after having Kye arrested, the victims decided that it would be healthy to drop charges.

Most of the man's arrests on gambling charges had been dismissed for insufficient evidence, but he had three misdemeanor convictions. He had paid modest fines in each case and had never served any time.

"This small-time hood can't be the one we're looking for," Linc said. "He wouldn't have brains enough to mastermind a deal like this."

Julie said, "He could be working for someone with brains enough to mastermind it."

After thinking this over, both boys nodded. Pete said, "That sounds more likely, if he is the Eddie Kye the Evans girl mentioned."

The suspect's mug shots showed a coarse-featured, beetle-browed man with a sullen expression. He was described as five feet eight and as weighing 205 pounds. His last-known address was listed as apartment 204 in an apartment building at Eighth and Hoover.

Pete wrote down the address and returned the manila envelope to its proper place on the shelf. Then the three of them returned to the R. and I. counter. Pete asked the girl behind the counter for a phone book.

A phone was listed under Kye, E. H., at the Eighth and Hoover address.

"So far, so good," Pete said. "Now let's see if the phone's still connected. You'd better do the checking out, Julie. Make like you're a magazine solicitor or something."

Nodding, Julie picked up the phone lying on the counter and dialed for an outside line. While Pete held his finger beneath the telephone number in order to mark it, she read it off to the operator.

On the third ring, a brusque male voice answered, "Yeah?"

"Mr. Kye?" Julie asked.

"Yeah."

"I'm calling for the Wholesale Magazine Institute, Mr. Kye," Julie said with deliberately false brightness. "I want to congratulate you on being one of a select local group chosen to receive, absolutely free, except for a modest handling charge, subscriptions to any three magazines of your choice. This introductory offer . . ."

The man broke in with disgust. "Who you trying to con, toots? I don't want no magazines and I don't want no more phone calls from you boiler-room operators. So blast off."

He hung up. Julie made a face and hung up.

"He's not a very charming gentleman, but he still lives there," she said.

"Good," Pete said. "If he does turn out to be the Eddie Kye we want, we'll know where to locate him."

Promptly at nine the next morning, Julie arrived at the Athletic Administration Building. She found the athletic director's office without difficulty.

The outer office was about thirty feet square. Against the left wall was a solid bank of file cabinets. Directly across from the door, in front of a pair of windows, were two long tables. One contained a mimeograph machine, a paper cutter and an adding machine. The other was piled with various publications, stacks of mimeographed material, graphs and charts and a stack of carbon copies of letters on canary-colored second sheets.

Centered in the right wall was a glass-paned door with lettering on it reading: ATHLETIC DIRECTOR, then below it, in smaller letters: Mark Doyle. Shelves against the wall on the near side of the door were loaded with what looked like reference works. Similar shelves the other side contained office supplies.

In the center of the room was a desk with a swivel chair. Next to it was a typewriter stand with an electric typewriter. A posture chair went with the stand.

Seated in the swivel chair with his feet on top of the desk was a handsome, leanly-muscled man in his late twenties with a blond crew cut and twinkling blue eyes. He was dressed in green slacks and a bright-yellow sport shirt with matching yellow socks.

The man swung his feet from the desk and came erect when Julie entered the room. He was quite tall, she noted, perhaps six feet two, and must have weighed around 190.

"Good morning," he said in a pleasant, rather resonant voice, showing strong white teeth in a smile. "Nobody's here yet, but maybe I can help you."

"More likely I can help you," Julie said, smiling back. "I'm Mr. Doyle's new secretary."

"Oh?" he said, appraising her with an admiring eye. "You'll see a lot of me, then. I'm Baldwin Hills' track coach."

"How do you do?" Julie said. "My name is Julie Barnes."

"Glad to know you, Julie. I'm Barney Kuehn. Professor Kuehn to the students, but Barney to fellow employees of this institution of higher learning."

Julie looked surprised. "Aren't most coaches called 'coach' by the kids?"

"Oh, sure, by the athletes. But the track season won't start for some time, and meanwhile I teach history. All the coaches here are teachers and just coach as extra assignments. The only full-time employee of the Athletic Department, aside from you, who has no duties outside of it, is your boss."

The athletic director walked in at that moment. "Morning, Julie," he said, glancing with approval at her neat white blouse and the plain blue skirt that came just to her knees. "Morning, Barney. Have you two met?"

"We introduced ourselves," Kuehn said.

"Good. I'll be with you as soon as I brief Julie on her duties." He turned to the girl. "The most urgent problem is the files. Quite frankly, I don't understand them at all. The first thing I want you to do is make a study of the filing system, so that you'll be able to put your hands on documents I want, without searching through everything in the cabinets."

"Yes, sir," Julie said.

Doyle walked over to the tables by the window and pointed to the stack of yellow second sheets. "The second thing I want you to do is to file these. They're carbons of letters I've written in the past couple of weeks, and I was afraid they'd disappear forever, if I tried to file them."

"I'll take care of it," Julie said, smiling.

Doyle took a key ring from his pocket, went over to the door of his private office and unlocked it.

"Come on in, Barney," he said.

When the two men had disappeared into the inner office, Julie deposited her handbag in a bottom drawer of the desk and went over to the bank of file cabinets. It didn't take her long to grasp the intricacies of the filing system, because her last undercover assignment had been as a file clerk.

There was a separate cabinet for each sport, plus one devoted to general matters. Within each category, the decimal system of filing by subject matter was used. A set of code books for the system stood upright between bookends on top of the cabinets.

The previous secretary seemed to have left the files in neat and orderly condition. Julie didn't contemplate any difficulty in using them, although she could understand how someone like Mark Doyle, unfamiliar with filing procedures, could get totally confused by the decimal system.

After she finished examining the files, Julie carried the stack of yellow carbon copies of letters to her desk, sat in the swivel chair and began reading the letters. As she finished each, she wrote its category and subject in light pencil in the upper lefthand corner. Later, she would look up the code number for each subject and also jot those down, after which she would place the sheets in their proper numerical places in the files.

She was still reading carbons and assigning them subjects, when Barney Kuehn emerged from the inner office. He paused before her desk.

"You have any plans for lunch, Julie?" he asked.

"Well, I thought I'd eat at the school cafeteria. I understand there is one in the Student Union."

"Sure," he said with a grin. "And it opens the same day school opens."

"Oh dear," Julie said. "I should have thought of that."

"No sweat," the track-coach-history-professor said. "There's a nice restaurant only a few blocks from here. I'll pick you up promptly at noon."

"Well . . ." she hesitated, her gaze straying to his left hand.

His grin widened. "No wedding ring, no wife, no fiancée, and not even a steady girl friend. I'm what hopeful mothers fondly refer to as an eligible bachelor."

"All right," she agreed, smiling back. "I'll expect you at noon."

Barney Kuehn had just left, when an intercom speaker on Julie's desk startled her. Mark Doyle's voice said, "Julie, take this down."

Examining the device, Julie saw that it contained three switches. One was merely an on-and-off switch, one was labeled *Speak*, the other *Receive*. The *Receive* button was depressed, she noted, and probably was supposed to be left that way on stand-by, so that the athletic director could simply speak to her when he wished to without first having to press his call buzzer.

Picking up a pencil and flicking open a notebook, Julie depressed the *Speak* button, said, "Go ahead, sir," and switched back to *Receive*.

Doyle said, "I want you to look up the score sheets on three track meets of last year. February 14 with Ventura Junior College, March 7 with Moorpark and March 28 with Valley State. Got that?"

"Yes, sir," Julie said.

Mark Doyle looked astonished when Julie entered his office about thirty seconds later and laid the three score sheets on his desk.

"How'd you find those so fast?" he inquired.

"The files are really in excellent condition," she said. "You just have to understand them."

"Well, I'm glad somebody around here does," he said. "I sure couldn't find anything in them."

Julie said, "Aren't those the meets that the Evans girl told you were fixed?"

"Uh-huh. I wanted to check Scooter Miller's times."

"Did you decide to take Professor Kuehn into your confidence about the bribes?"

Doyle raised his eyebrows. "Oh, no. Dr. Vester specifically instructed me to tell no one but the police. Barney was here on an entirely different matter."

"Oh," Julie said. "Then he's unaware that I'm a cop."

"Completely."

"Fine," she said with a smile. "That makes things less complicated."

She returned to the outer office and went back to work.

CHAPTER 4

BALDWIN HILLS College had a total enrollment of about three-thousand, approximately half men and half women. Only about five-hundred men and five-hundred women lived in each of the two dormitories, however. About half the students were residents of the greater Los Angeles area and lived at home. The remaining five hundred lived in off-campus rooming houses or shared apartments with other students.

Howard Wayne Hall, named after an early college president, was the official name of the men's dormitory. It was a two-story brick building with an arched front entrance and heavy double doors that would have been more appropriate for a medieval castle. Immediately inside was a long counter resembling a hotel reservation desk, where a student clerk was on duty.

An archway to the right of this counter led into a large lobby furnished with sofas, easy chairs, card tables, a baby grand piano and a color TV set. A similar archway to the left led along a short hallway to a curtained glass door, which looked as though it might be the entrance to an apartment.

The building was divided into two wings, with sixty-four double rooms on each floor of each wing. There were connecting baths between each pair of rooms, so that there was a bathroom for each four students.

Just inside the front entrance on either side of the door, stone staircases angled upward and also downward to the basement. The basement contained the dining hall, a dispensary and the heating plant.

As Labor Day happened to fall on September 1st, Tuesday the 2nd was registration day. Pete and Linc checked into the dormitory Labor Day afternoon about four, as Mark Doyle had told them most students checked in a day early, in order to be on hand early on registration day.

The student clerk on duty was a lanky youngster who looked no more than eighteen. He located their names on a chart, then removed two keys from one of the numerous pigeonholes that covered the entire wall behind the counter and gave one to each boy.

"You fellows lived here before?" he asked.

When the boys said no, the clerk said, "Well, 244 is up that staircase." He pointed to the one on the left as you entered the building. "That wing is all upperclassmen. The other is all freshmen and sophomores."

The boys thanked him and went back outside to get their luggage from the Woody, which they had left parked in the fifteen-minute loading zone in front.

The vehicle the Mod Squad affectionately called the Woody was their officially assigned police car. It was a station wagon with a rack on top to which a surfboard was usually strapped. Instead of hanging in plain view, the microphone of the station wagon's two-way radio was under the dashboard, where it couldn't be seen even by a passenger in the front seat.

The boys had each brought along a suitcase plus a Val-pack. When they had unloaded them onto the sidewalk, Linc offered to carry all four pieces inside, while Pete drove the Woody to the parking lot in front of the dormitory.

"Okay," Pete said. "Just leave my stuff in front of the counter."

After parking the station wagon, Pete reentered the building. He found his luggage where he had told Linc to leave it and carried it up to the second floor. Linc had left the door to room 244 open. When Pete carried his bags in, Linc had both his suitcase and Val-pack on one of the twin beds. The suitcase was open, and he was transferring underwear and socks to one of the twin dressers.

The room, about twenty-five feet square, was well lighted by a single wide window that took up about a third of the length of the outer wall. In addition to the twin beds and dressers, the only other furnishings were two writing desks with student lamps and two straight-backed chairs. While the furniture showed some wear, it was of good, solid quality and gave the room an attractive appearance. There were individual closets on each side of the door.

When both boys had finished unpacking and had stowed their luggage in the backs of their closets, Pete went over to open the door of the bath connecting with the room next to theirs. The door on the opposite side was open, and while Pete could not see anyone in the other room, he could hear the sound of conversation coming from there. One male voice wondered aloud if "the girls" had as yet checked into the girls' dorm, presumably meaning some specific girls. A deeper voice suggested they check as soon as they finished unpacking.

Mark Doyle had informed Pete and Linc that he had managed to get them assigned to the room whose bath connected with that of Scooter Miller and his roommate. Therefore, one of the voices might be that of the bribe-taking track star. Pete glanced at Linc in silent inquiry as to whether they should move in at once or let the occupants of the other room discover them.

Linc passed the decision back by shrugging. Deciding to make the first move, Pete walked through the bathroom and glanced into the other room. Linc trailed after him and peered over his shoulder.

The two occupants of the other room were hanging clothes in their closets. Both glanced over their shoulders when Pete said, "Hi."

Both boys appeared to be around twenty-one. The larger, who was at least six feet three and probably weighed close to 250 pounds, had a rugged, good-natured face and close-cropped flaming red hair. The other one was about Linc's size and build, but had Pete's general coloring, with light-brown hair and green eyes. He was exceptionally handsome, with even features and liquid, long-lashed eyes that many women probably envied, but which failed to seem feminine on him because he exuded such a strong air of masculinity.

The smaller youth said, "Hello. You fellows sharing our bath with us?"

"Uh-huh," Pete said.

The big redhead closed his closet door and turned to face Pete and Linc. He said, "I don't remember seeing you guys in the dorm last year. You new around here?"

Linc said, "We're transfers from Central College back in Missouri."

The smaller youth also closed his closet door and advanced with his hand extended.

"I'm Lloyd Miller," he announced with a welcoming smile. "Generally called Scooter."

Pete accepted the handclasp, told his own name and introduced Linc. After shaking hands with Linc also, Scooter Miller introduced his roommate as Larry Coons, then added with a wicked grin that Larry was a nickname, too.

When Linc innocently asked, "For what?" Coons' face reddened, and he gazed at Miller belligerently.

"I can never remember," Scooter said. "Lawrence, I think. Isn't it Lawrence, Larry?"

Coons continued to stare at him belligerently until the smaller man grinned and said, "He doesn't like to be called Lawrence. You'll have to remember to call him Larry. Otherwise he pouts."

The big redhead's belligerence disappeared, and he said with an odd tinge of relief in his voice, "Lloyd isn't such a hot name either, comedian."

Pete got the strange impression that the relief stemmed from his roommate's implication that his real name was Lawrence, which suggested that it wasn't. It seemed obvious that it was something he was ashamed of.

Scooter Miller said, "You fellows just get in town?"

"Uh-huh," Pete said.

"Ever visit the campus before?"

Pete shook his head.

"Well, as soon as we finish unpacking, Larry and I will introduce you to some of the guys and show you around the school. Okay?"

"Fine with us," Pete said.

"We'll only be about fifteen minutes, probably. You can squat on the beds and wait, if you like."

Pete said, "We've got one or two things still to put away ourselves. Give a yell when you're ready."

"Sure," the track man said, and walked over to an open suitcase to begin lifting clothes out of it.

Pete and Linc returned to their room, and Pete pulled the bathroom door closed behind them.

"What do you think Larry's really a nickname for?" he asked Linc.

"You caught that too, huh?" Linc said with a grin. "My guess is something like Laverne or Llewellyn. Whatever it is, he doesn't want it out."

A quarter of an hour later a rap came on the bathroom door. When Pete called, "Come in," the door opened, and Scooter Miller and Larry Coons came in. Both had previously been in shirt sleeves, but now had slipped on light jackets. Since it was about seventy-five degrees outside, Pete and Linc examined them with some surprise.

Catching their expressions, Scooter said, "Larry and I probably won't roll back in until after midnight. And it cools off after dark."

Pete and Linc exchanged glances, tacitly decided to stick with the pair as long as they were welcome and put on light jackets, too.

All four moved out into the hall, Pete locking the door behind them. The door directly across the hall was open, and a tall, gangling blond youth of about twenty lay on one of the beds. A stocky Mexican-American of about the same age stood gazing out the window.

The blond youth said, "Hey there, Scooter. Hi yuh, Larry."

The Mexican-American turned around, grinned and said, "Well, look who we drew for neighbors."

Scooter and Larry threw back friendly greetings. Scooter steered Pete and Linc into the room ahead of him. Larry Coons remained in the doorway.

"These are some new guys who transferred in from some college in Missouri," Scooter announced. He gave Pete an inquiring look. "I never asked you as what."

"Juniors," Pete said.

Scooter introduced the tall boy, who towered to about six feet seven when he unfolded his lanky frame from the bed, as Art Feister, adding the information that he was last year's captain of the basketball team. The stocky Mexican-American was called Cesar Ramirez.

Scooter gave Pete and Linc no chance to get acquainted with the pair, despite the cordiality of his introduction. As soon as everyone had shaken hands, he shooed Pete and Linc out of the room again, commenting that they had too much ground to cover to linger.

The quartet moved on, Scooter glancing through each open door and pausing to introduce Pete and Linc to the occupants in most cases. Some he passed by, though. Most of these seemed to be students he didn't know, since he moved past without greeting them. But in a few cases he threw a casual greeting or an even more casual wave without breaking stride. Presumably these were boys he knew but didn't regard as important enough to introduce to his new friends. He also didn't bother to knock on any doors that weren't open.

Miller's and Coons' room, number 246, was at the far end of the hall from the stairway, next to the fire door, and 244 was the second farthest on that side of the hall. There was a phone on the wall halfway between the stairs and the fire door. They had worked their way even with it when it started to ring. Scooter Miller answered it.

"Upperclass second," he said.

After listening, he said, "Hold on," and let the receiver dangle by its cord. Raising his voice, he yelled, "Arnie Trotter!"

A door near the stairway opened. A skinny young man with shoulder-length, straw-colored hair and a Fu Manchu moustache peered out.

"Phone," Scooter called.

The quartet again began to move toward the stairs as the moustached Arnie Trotter approached and passed them. As he went by, he threw a curt, unfriendly, "Thanks," at Scooter Miller, gave Larry Coons an indifferent nod and ignored Pete and Linc.

"What's bugging him?" Pete asked when he had gone by.

"Arnie's the leader of the local SDS," Miller said. "He regards me and Larry as members of the Establishment."

Linc said, "Students for a Democractic Society, you mean? Are they active here?"

"You better believe it. We also have an Afro-American Student Union which stages regular protests. As a matter of fact, its president roomed with Trotter last year."

At that moment, a slender black youth wearing a small, pointed goatee and a thin moustache appeared in the doorway Arnie Trotter had emerged from and glanced their way.

Miller said, "Looks like he's rooming with him again this year."

The slender black youth's eyes widened in surprise when he saw Linc Hayes.

Approaching with his right hand outstretched, he said, "Linc, baby! What the devil are you doing here?"

CHAPTER 5

LINC's initial reaction, when he recognized the bearded black youth as an old high-school friend, was consternation at having his cover blown. Then he realized that as he hadn't been in contact with Dewey Stockton since high-school days, there was no reason he couldn't bluff his way through.

Cordially grasping the extended hand, he said, "Good to see you, Dewey. I'm doing the same thing here you are. I'm a junior here."

"Yeah?" Stockton said in a surprised voice. "Last I heard, you were in the can for tossing firebombs during one of the riots down in our old neighborhood. I thought you would have worked your way to San Quentin by now."

"Good old Dewey," Linc said, grinning. "Always wishing the best for everybody." He examined the youth's beard and moustache, which gave his somewhat thin face a marked satanic appearance, and let his grin widen. "Since you grew that fuzz, has anyone told you that you look like the devil? I don't mean you look bad. I mean literally like the guy who runs Hades."

Dewey Stockton made a face. "Your puns aren't getting any better, Linc. No fooling, you've been here at school all along, without me running into you before?"

"Not here," Linc said. "I put in two years at Central College back in Missouri and just transferred here now."

"Oh? Do any running back there?"

Linc offered silent thanks that he had done enough running in high school to make his supposed track record in college sound believable. He said, "Uh-huh. I've managed to cut my old slow time on the hundred to 9.6, and to heave the javelin 230."

Scooter Miller interrupted to say, "You're a track man, Linc?"

"Uh-huh. Pete too. He's a jumper. Dewey, meet my buddy Pete Cochrane, who just transferred from Central too. This is Dewey Stockton, Pete, an old high-school pal of mine from Watts."

As the two shook hands, Miller said to Linc, "How come you went clear off to Missouri to school if you're from Watts?"

"Got an uncle back there," Linc said easily. "And my folks thought he might be able to straighten me out. You heard what Dewey said about the trouble I was in. I used to be kind of a juvenile delinquent. After two years of Uncle Bert's supervision, I've been decreed reformed enough to return home."

"Your folks still live in Watts?"

Linc had anticipated the question. He said, "Yeah, but I'm one of eleven kids and there's only one bathroom. I got too used to elbow room to move back home."

Miller glanced at Pete. "How come he transferred here, too? Or is he from around here, too?" There was no suspicion in his voice. Obviously he was merely curious.

Linc sidestepped the second question and merely answered the first. "He's my buddy. I talked him into it."

The answer seemed to satisfy Scooter Miller.

Arnie Trotter returned from his phone call at that moment and was introduced to Linc and Pete by Stockton. He shook hands with both cordially enough but virtually ignored Scooter Miller and Larry Coons. Dewey Stockton had barely acknowledged the pair's presence either, both Pete and Linc noted, merely giving them each a polite nod.

As soon as the SDS leader had shaken hands with Pete and Linc, Scooter Miller said, "We'd better move on, if you guys want to see everything."

Pete nodded, and Linc said, "Okay, Scooter. Dewey, come see us. We're in room 244."

"Sure. Drop by and see us too, Linc. I'll split open some wine I've got stashed away."

Pete and Linc moved on with Miller and Coons, as the other two reentered their room. Scooter halted again after moving only a few feet, and the other three halted also to look at him inquiringly.

The track star said to Pete, "What do you jump?"

"Both the high jump and the long jump."

"Oh?" Scooter said. "How good are you?"

"Not very," Pete said modestly. "Six-seven on the high jump and twenty-three and a half on the long jump."

Scooter looked impressed. "Hey, that's good enough to win points in this league." He turned to Linc. "Did I hear you say you ran the hundred in 9.6 and threw the javelin 230?"

"Uh-huh."

"You can compete in this league, too. My record sprint is only 9.5, and I'm supposed to be tops in the conference."

"Oh, you're a sprinter, too?" Linc asked innocently.

Big Larry Coons, who had hardly opened his mouth other than to say hello to students he knew, emitted a deep-voiced chuckle. "Why do you think they call him Scooter?" he inquired.

Miller dropped a hand on his roommate's chunky shoulder and said, "Larry's pretty good too. He holds the school record for both shot put and discus throw. But, basically, his sport is football. He's first-string offensive fullback."

Pete and Linc both looked suitably impressed.

The four of them continued on, stopping at a couple of more rooms with open doors to meet students, then descending the stairs. Scooter glanced up at the clock over the counter where the student clerk was on duty.

"Hey, it's 5 P.M.," he said. "We'd better skip introducing you guys to first-floor residents until tomorrow or we won't have time to show you around the campus. Larry, shall we buzz the girls' dorm to see if the girls have checked in yet?"

"Yeah, let's," the big redhead said.

Miller led the way into the lobby, where there were three phone booths against the far wall. As they crossed toward them, Miller explained that up until midnight, after which there was no clerk on duty to run the switchboard, students could receive phone calls on the wall phones in the halls of both wings, but that those phones could be used for outgoing calls only for emergencies. All ordinary outgoing calls had to be made from the pay phones.

The track star closed himself in one of the booths while the others waited. He was there a very short time.

When he emerged, he said, "They both just checked in a few minutes ago. They're probably unpacking, so I told the girl not to bother them. We'll stop by after awhile."

"Okay," Coons said agreeably.

While Miller had decided there wasn't time to introduce his new friends to any more students, he did take a few more minutes to point out one or two things about the building. As Pete and Linc had suspected, the curtained glass door to the left of the counter did lead into an apartment. The dormitory manager and his wife, who had charge of the dining hall, lived there.

"Old Pop and Mom Henderson have been here about twenty-five years, I guess," Scooter told them. "They must both be around sixty. He used to have the title of dormitory father years back, but they changed it to dormitory manager when practically all the rules were scrapped. At the girls' dorm they still have a midnight curfew on weeknights and a 2 A.M. curfew on weekends, but in Howard Wayne Hall we come and go as we please. Years back, I guess Pop used to break up crap games in the rooms, but the new rules bar him from entering any student room without invitation."

"Sounds pretty swinging," Pete said.

"Oh, it's going to get swingier. This year, I understand the guys are going to agitate for the right to have girls in their rooms whenever they want."

"What guys?" Pete asked.

"Various protest groups."

"Like the SDS and the Afro-American Student Union?" Linc asked.

"Well, not them so much. They tend to consider those kind of demands frivolous. They go after stuff like getting a voice in appointing and firing professors and having courses run the way they want them instead of the way the profs want them. We've got dozens of student movements ready to break out signs at the drop of a hat for anything from the right to wear Bermuda shorts to class to the right to bar Navy recruiters from the campus."

Pete asked, "How do you feel about all this student protest?"

Miller shrugged. "Some of it's justified. Particularly the reforms the black guys have gone after, because black students weren't getting anything close to a fair shake, until they stood up on their hind feet and started demanding reforms. But a lot of it's nonsense. I don't get involved in any of it."

Pete glanced at Larry Coons who said, "Me neither. I'm here to get a degree and maybe a pro football contract. You won't see me carrying any picket signs."

Scooter Miller abruptly changed the subject by saying, "Come on, and I'll show you the basement."

He led them downstairs for a quick look into the dispensary and the dining hall. The dining hall would open for breakfast in the morning, he told them, but tonight they had to eat out.

That ended the tour of the dormitory. Miller and Coons proceeded to show them the rest of the campus.

The campus proper, exclusive of the athletic field, which was separate from it, was the equivalent of a city block wide on its north and south borders and three blocks long the other way. At the far south end was a parking lot for visitors and students who lived off campus. Just north of it was the administration building, whose official name was Rogers Memorial Hall. It was a two-story brick building with wide stone steps leading up to it from the parking lot. At the top of the steps, an arched passageway ran through the center of the building to a quadrangle on the other side of the building.

The quadrangle was formed by the administration building and three other buildings. To the north was the school library, whose front door faced south and which was the same length as Rogers Memorial Hall, although it was only one story tall. To the west, the liberal arts building extended from a point only about six feet from the corner of the administration building to within six feet of the library. Directly across from the liberal arts building, at the east edge of the campus, the school chapel formed the fourth side of the quadrangle.

The area enclosed by the four buildings was about fifty yards square. Sidewalks crossed it diagonally, and one also ran from the arched passageway cutting through the administration building to the library. There were a number of stone benches on the grassed area, all of them well shaded by towering trees.

"Here's where you take your date to make out, if you haven't got a car," Scooter Miller told Pete and Linc. "Except for a light in that archway and another on the library veranda, there's no light at all here at night. And the trees keep those benches in pitch-dark shadow."

"We'll keep it in mind, but we have a car," Pete said. "Or, rather, a station wagon."

North of the library were grouped all the class buildings other than the liberal arts building. Beyond the last, which happened to be the science building, were the two dormitories, the girls' on the west edge of the campus, the boys' on the east edge. The parking lot for both, also used by the faculty and other school employees, was between them.

North of the dormitory parking lot was the Student Union, which also contained the faculty lounge.

Beyond that was the Athletic Administration Building. The field houses and the gym were at the very north edge of the campus.

The athletic field was separated from the rest of the campus by the street running along the campus' east edge and was directly across the street from the field house.

The conducted tour ended up in front of the girls' dormitory. Scooter Miller asked Pete what time it was.

When Pete checked his watch and told him it was a quarter of six, Miller said to his red-haired roommate, "The girls should be organized by now." Then he said to Pete and Linc, "Come on and we'll introduce you to our girl friends."

CHAPTER 6

THE inside of the girls' dormitory was arranged exactly like the men's dorm. Scooter Miller asked the girl on duty behind the counter to inform Barbara Fenton and Patricia Lathrop that they had visitors in the lobby.

While the clerk was phoning, the four boys went through the archway to the right of the counter to wait in the lobby. No one else was there. Pete and Linc sank into leather-covered chairs, but apparently the other two were too excited at the prospect of seeing their girl friends again to sit. They both preferred to pace back and forth.

A few minutes later, two slim young girls in slacks and sweaters came into the lobby together. One had close-cropped, brick-red hair and a span of freckles across her cute pug nose. The other was a glamorous-looking platinum blonde.

When the girls spotted Miller and Coons, they ran the rest of the way and threw themselves into the boys' arms, the blonde picking Scooter Miller and the red-head choosing his oversized roommate. Pete and Linc rose to their feet and studied the girls with interest as they greeted their boyfriends with enthusiastic kisses.

Glancing from Larry Coons's flaming red hair to his girl friend's equally bright shock, Linc said to Pete in a whispered aside, "If Larry ever marries that gal, they're going to have the reddest-haired kids anybody ever saw."

Pete gave a smiling nod.

When Miller and Coons recovered from this pleasant but violent welcome, they introduced the blonde as Barbara Fenton and the redhead as Patty Lathrop. The girls acknowledged the introductions politely enough, but they were both too happy to be reunited with their boyfriends to give anyone else much attention. Immediately, both turned back to their boyfriends, and a running four-way dialogue ensued about what all four had been doing since they last saw each other.

In the course of the conversation, Pete and Linc gathered that, while Barbara and Scooter Miller had been separated for only a few weeks because both had attended summer school, Patty and Larry Coons hadn't seen each other since the end of the regular school year the previous June. It seemed that both girls were from San Diego, while Scooter Miller was from Bakersfield and Coons was from Fresno. The girls announced that they were rooming together this year, and from the pleased reaction of the boys, it seemed apparent that they hadn't been roommates the previous year. Pete and Linc gathered that, while the two girls had known each other in San Diego even before attending Baldwin Hills College, they had become close friends only since Barbara became the steady girl of the roommate of Patty's steady.

It also emerged from the conversation that both girls were sophomores this year, while their boyfriends were both seniors.

When everyone had finally been brought up-to-date on the others' vacation activities, Scooter said, "What are you gals doing about dinner tonight?"

The brick-topped Patty said, "My folks drove us up and are staying overnight at the Statler. They're picking me and Barb up to take us to dinner in about half an hour. If you two want to come along, I'm sure Dad won't mind."

"Oh, no," Larry Coons said. "Your dad spooks me."

Patty frowned at him. "You only met him once, when he came to pick me up last June. How could he spook you?"

"That's when he spooked me," the big redhead said. "He fixed me with those gimlet eyes of his, and I could see him wondering what right a muscle-bound dunce like me had courting his only daughter."

"Oh, don't be silly. Dad really liked you."

"Then why'd he look at me like that?"

The blonde Barbara giggled. "Because Patty's his only daughter, Larry. He'll never fully approve of any boy for Patty. But from remarks he made this summer whenever the subject of you came up, I think he detests you less than any boy she ever brought around before."

This news didn't seem to make the fullback feel any better. In fact, he looked faintly alarmed. After examining his expression Patty said to the blonde in an indignant tone, "Now you've fixed things so he'll never go near Dad."

Scooter Miller said diplomatically, "Why don't we all meet at the Petöfi Club after dinner? You could have your father drop you and Barb off there, Patty."

"But don't tell him who you're meeting," Larry Coons said quickly.

Patty frowned at him again, but decided to ignore the remark. She said to Scooter, "All right. We should be able to make it by nine."

Miller said, "Maybe we'll take you girls nightclubbing."

"Hey, speak for yourself," Coons said. "I'm almost flat."

"Well, so am I at the moment, but I think I may be able to raise enough for one final blast before we settle down to study. If I can't, you gals will have to be content with Cokes at the Petöfi Club. We'll let you know when you get there."

"Either's all right with me," Patty said, gazing up into Coons' face, this time with a fond smile instead of with a frown. "Just so I'm with Larry. I love the big lug."

Larry Coons' face turned as red as his hair.

After a few more minutes of conversation, to which Pete and Linc continued merely to listen, the girls announced that they had to go dress for dinner. Then both girls simultaneously seemed to realize they had been ignoring the newcomers, and both offered rueful apologies.

Pete said, "That's all right, girls. We understand," and Linc said with a grin. "Don't worry about it. We enjoyed watching Larry's panic over Patty's father."

Coons glowered at Linc, but Scooter Miller laughed. "It's not panic, Linc, just extreme caution."

"It's neither," Coons denied. "He just spooks me, is all."

It was after six when the four boys left the girls' dorm. Miller suggested that they all have dinner at some nearby restaurant, then go together to the Petöfi Club.

"What is that place?" Pete asked.

"Just a student hangout," the track star told him. "No booze; just sodas and sundaes and snacks. It's run by a refugee from the Hungarian uprising, who named it after a poet and hero of the 1848 Hungarian Revolution named Sándor Petöfi."

Because Scooter and Larry had dates and might want to take them somewhere other than the Petöfi Club, they decided to take two cars. It developed that Scooter Miller owned a four-year-old Pontiac sedan. He and his roommate rode in that, while Pete and Linc followed in the Woody.

Scooter led them to a small restaurant a few blocks from the campus, where they had a fair meal at reasonable prices. They dined unhurriedly, and it was nearly eight when they all arrived at the Petöfi Club, which was only two blocks from the campus.

The name of the place turned out to be the only exotic thing about it. It was merely a dairy bar, with booths all around the walls and with formica-topped tables in the center. It seemed to be a favorite student hangout, though, because it was packed with young people, many of whom wore school sweaters or sweat shirts.

In one of the booths near the door, an attractive brunette and an equally attractive black girl sat across from each other. The brunette was an exceptionally pretty girl, with finely-chiseled features, a voluptuous mouth and a pale complexion. The black girl had a sensual, high-cheekboned face, flashing black eyes and flawless, gleaming, black skin. Both girls were somewhere around five feet four or five and had slender but well-formed figures. Both were dressed in miniskirts and white blouses, with light sweaters over the blouses. They both appeared to be in their late teens.

Larry Coons gave the girls a wide smile and said, "Hi, Eve. How are you, Althea?"

Scooter Miller spoke to both girls, too, but he didn't call them by name, and his tone was oddly reserved. He merely nodded to them and said, "Hi there."

The black girl replied to both greetings courteously enough, but the other girl returned only Larry Coons' greeting and completely ignored Scooter Miller. The track star hurried on by to a vacant booth at the right side of the room. When they reached the booth, Miller told his roommate to slide in next to the wall, as he had to get out to make a phone call as soon as they had ordered. Coons took the side of the booth that would make him face the front door. Pete sat next to the wall on the other side, and Linc sat next to him.

"Who are those girls you spoke to?" Pete asked, when they were all settled.

Larry Coons said, "The black girl is Althea Moore. The other is Eve Evans. They're both juniors, and they were roommates last year. Probably again this year, too, since they're together."

"Any chance of meeting them?" Pete asked.

"Not from me," Scooter said shortly.

Before either Pete or Linc could inquire why not, a plump, middle-aged woman, wearing an apron and speaking with a pronounced Hungarian accent, came to take their orders. They all ordered small Cokes.

As the woman moved away, Miller said, "That's Magda, the proprietor's wife. His name's Janos, and he's the guy with the moustache behind the soda fountain."

Pete and Linc turned to gaze at the burly man in a white jacket, who was working behind the counter. Scooter rose and dropped a dollar bill on the tabletop.

"I'll pop for the Cokes," he said. "Get them out of that, Larry. Be back in a minute."

He made for a phone booth on the opposite side of the room.

Pete said to Coons, "What's Scooter's grudge against those girls you spoke to?"

"None against Althea," the big redhead said. "But he used to go steady with Eve before he ran into Barb this summer. She doesn't speak to him since the break-up."

"Oh," Pete said. "No wonder he didn't want to introduce us."

Their Cokes were delivered, Larry paid for them with the bill Scooter had left and let the change lie on the table. A few moments later, Scooter returned.

"We're in," he said to Coons, as he slid into the booth. "We're going to be able to show the girls a real blast."

For the next twenty minutes, the four of them sat and conversed and sipped their Cokes. Scooter and Larry periodically waved or called greetings to students they recognized at other tables, and a number of boys came over to the booth to greet the pair and be introduced to Pete and Linc. It seemed apparent that both boys were extremely popular with fellow students.

Then Scooter, who had been closely watching the door, suddenly rose to his feet, with a pleased smile on his face. "Be back," he said, and headed that way.

Pete and Linc glanced over their shoulders just in time to see the man who had poked his head in the door back out and let the door close behind him again. The man wasn't very tall, but his chunky, powerfully-built body must have weighed over two-hundred pounds.

Both Pete and Linc recognized the coarse-featured, beetle-browed face. The expression wasn't as sullen as it had been in the mug shots; in fact, it was quite cheerful. But there was no doubt that it belonged to the Edgar H. Kye whose record they had studied at the Golden Horseshoe.

CHAPTER 7

SCOOTER MILLER went past the booth where Eve Evans and Althea Moore sat, without glancing at the girls. As he disappeared through the front door, the black girl rose from her seat and went to get a package of cigarettes from a machine at the rear of the room. She circled around the opposite side of a row of tables parallel to the line of booths where the boys were seated en route to the machine, but returned by the aisle between the tables and the booths.

As she neared their booth, Linc said in a low voice to Larry, "With Scooter gone you can introduce us to this chick, can't you?"

The big redhead, who was seated with his back to the approaching girl, glanced over his shoulder. "Sure," he said agreeably.

As the black girl came abreast of them, he said, "Hey, Althea, stop and meet some friends of mine."

Halting, Althea turned to face the booth. When Linc started to slide out of it in order to rise to his feet, she placed a restraining hand on his shoulder.

"These booths are too hard to get in and out of," she said with a smile. "It's accepted custom at the Petöfi Club that boys don't stand when girls stop at their booths."

With a shrug, Linc settled back in his seat. Larry Coons introduced him and Pete, then added the information that they were new transferees and were both juniors.

"Oh?" she said, looking at Linc. "From where?"

"Central College, at Fayette, Missouri."

Apparently, she had never heard of it, because the name brought no reaction. After a moment or two more of polite conversation, the girl held up the package of cigarettes she had just bought and said, "I have to get back to my booth. These are community property and Eve's probably waiting for one. Nice to have met you fellows."

Pete and Linc told her they were glad to have met her, also. Althea returned to her own booth, and a moment later Scooter Miller came back inside. He sat next to his oversized roommate.

"We'll be able to give the girls a real bash," he said in a smug voice, briefly displaying a fifty-dollar bill, then thrusting it into his pocket. "I got an advance against future services."

Big Larry Coons frowned at him. "I don't want to know about it," he said. "I don't mind helping you spend it, but keep quiet about how you earn it."

Pete and Linc glanced at each other and tacitly agreed not to follow up on this tempting opening. It would have sounded quite natural to inquire as to what the other two were talking about, probably. But both knew it was too soon to expect confidences from either Scooter Miller or his roommate, and there was no point in risking possible suspicion by asking a question that wasn't going to get a truthful answer, anyway. They deliberately ignored the exchange.

Promptly at 9 P.M., Barbara Fenton and Patty Lathrop appeared, both in ordinary street dresses and thin cloth coats. When the girls stopped just inside the door and gazed around, Scooter and Larry immediately got out of the booth.

"There's our dates," Scooter said. "See you guys."

He and Coons went to meet the girls and ushered them right back out. Eve Evans' gaze smoldered after them.

"Shall we move in on Eve and Althea?" Linc suggested to Pete.

"Sure," Pete said. "It's in the line of duty."

Both had long since finished their Cokes, so they left the empty glasses there. Linc led the way over to the booth where the girls sat.

"Our buddies ran out on us," he said to Althea. "Mind if we join you?"

"Of course not," the black girl said, moving over in her seat to make room. "Eve, this is Linc Hayes and Pete Cochrane. My roommate, Eve Evans, boys."

The boys both said they were glad to meet her. Eve murmured something vaguely polite, but her manner was cool, and she quite obviously was not enthusiastic about having the boys join them. She didn't invitingly move over to make room in the seat next to her, as Althea had.

Linc sat next to Althea. Pete remained standing, gazing down at Eve Evans without any particular expression on his face.

Finally, he said in a quiet tone, "I don't push myself on girls who don't like me, Eve, but if your grudge is that we were with your ex-boyfriend, we just met him a few hours ago."

The brunette gave him a startled look, then her eyes narrowed. "What did he say about me?" she demanded. "He must have said something or you wouldn't know we used to go together."

Pete shook his head. "He didn't even mention you. While he was away from our booth, I asked Larry Coons why you froze him. He said you and Scooter used to go steady, but have broken up. That's all Linc and I know about it, and all we want to know. But if you're going to freeze every guy who speaks to your ex-boyfriend, you won't be on speaking terms with half the student body. You want to thaw and move over, or you want me to blast off?"

After a moment of staring up at him wide-eyed, she gave him a repentant smile and slid over against the wall. "I'm sorry," she said. "I'm usually not so rude."

Giving her a smile of forgiveness, Pete sat next to her. "Let's drop it and start being friends," he suggested. "We can begin by you recounting your life history up to now." He examined her speculatively. "That would cover about nineteen years, wouldn't it?"

"Oh, come on," she said. "I'm a junior."

"Twenty?"

"Almost twenty-one. I wasn't very bright in high school, so I was nearly nineteen when I entered college." She nodded toward Althea. "She's the bright one. She'll graduate at nineteen. Althea is girl judo champ of Baldwin Hills in her weight class."

Linc and Pete both looked at the black girl in surprise.

"That doesn't mean much," Althea said dismissingly. "Only twenty-two girls went out last year, and only eight were in my weight class. There's no conference competition, you know. It's only an intramural program. Eve's as good as I am."

"Oh, come on," Eve said. "We're in the same weight class, and I came in third."

"Luck," the black girl said. "You know that when opponents are evenly matched, it's just luck as to who throws who. Coach Thorn even said so."

Pete and Linc looked at each other. "Our luck runs funny, too, doesn't it, buddy?" Pete said. "The two prettiest girls we've so far met around here have to turn out to be judo experts."

"Why should that matter if you behave yourselves?" Eve inquired.

"We didn't necessarily have behaving in mind," Pete said glumly.

Eve made a face at him, then said to her roommate, "Maybe we'll get a chance to use our training. I've never had a practical opportunity to use it."

Holding up both hands palm out, Linc said, "No contest. I concede in advance."

"You sure know how to spoil things," Althea complained to the milk-complexioned brunette. "Now they're afraid of us."

"Not really," Linc said, smiling at her. He glanced at the empty Coke glasses before the girls. "Would you gals like something to eat or drink?"

Eve screwed up her nose. "Not to eat. We're both on diets. And that was our second Coke. But the custom is to pay rent on your booth or table by ordering something at least every hour, and the rent on this booth is about due. We ought to order something, I suppose."

"No more iced drinks for me," Althea said. "I'll have a cup of coffee."

All four decided they would have coffee.

During the next hour, they exchanged histories and became thoroughly acquainted. Except for their mythical two years of college in Missouri and, of course, their connection with the LAPD, the boys stuck pretty much to the truth about their backgrounds. Eve said that she was an only child, and that her mother was a widow and worked as a telephone operator in San Francisco. Althea was from Oakland, where her father was a postman. She was the youngest of eight children, she told them, and was in school on a full scholarship.

"That's the only way I could have gone," the black girl said. "And without a summer job to take care of miscellaneous expenses not paid by the scholarship, I couldn't even have made it. A postman's salary doesn't stretch to higher education, when you've got eight kids."

"Yeah, I know," Linc said with rueful understanding. "My poor pop had to worry about eleven of us."

At ten o'clock, the girls suggested that they ought to get back to the girls' dorm, as they wanted to get up early for registration. When it developed that they had walked, the boys offered to drive them back to the dorm.

Pete parked the Woody in the loading zone in front of the girls' dorm long enough for him and Linc to walk to the front door. The two couples drifted apart to either side of the door for private conversation.

"See you again?" Pete asked Eve.

"If you'd like."

"Tomorrow night?"

"I usually don't go out on school nights," Eve said.

He cocked an eye at her. "To quote your favorite line, oh, come on. All you have to do tomorrow is register, then you could nap all afternoon, if you wanted to. You can't possibly have any homework until the day after tomorrow, because classes don't start until then."

"Well, I suppose registration day really doesn't count as a school day," she conceded. "What did you have in mind?"

"Maybe a little dancing?"

"All right," she agreed. "What time?"

"I'll phone you," Pete told her.

He didn't want to fix a time at that moment, because he thought that Linc might also be making a date with Althea. And he didn't want to call across to inquire if Linc was interested in going on a double, because that would put him on the spot, in case he wasn't interested in dating Althea.

It later developed that Linc had made a date with

Althea for the next night, and had left the time open for the same considerate reason.

When they got back to the men's dorm, Pete phoned Eve from one of the booths in the lobby and told her he and Linc would be by at eight the next evening.

CHAPTER 8

WHEN they registered, Pete and Linc deliberately chose courses taught by the various athletic coaches. Each registered for five three-day-a-week classes, or a total of fifteen semester hours of work.

Pete signed up for an advanced course in economics, because it was taught by the football coach. He also signed for a physics course taught by the basketball coach, a course in international relations taught by the swimming coach and a drama course taught by the tennis and golf coach.

By signing up for American literature, chemistry, botany and French, Linc drew as instructors the baseball coach, the archery coach, the head coach for intramural sports and the trainer for both football and basketball.

For their fifth course, both boys registered for medieval history under Professor Bernard Kuehn, the track coach.

By 11:30 A.M., Pete and Linc had finished registering and had nothing to do for the rest of the day. They decided to stop by to see Julie.

They got to the Athletic Administration Building just before noon and found Julie alone in the outer office of the athletic director's section. She glanced up from the letter she was typing when they came in, gave them a welcoming smile, and stopped typing in the middle of a sentence and swung her posture chair around to face them.

"How's it going?" Pete asked.

"All right," she said. "Except I don't seem to be accomplishing much aside from getting my secretarial work done. I've pored over the record of every athlete in school, but I don't understand what the captain expected me to find. It isn't going to show on his record if a man accepts bribes."

"Captain Greer isn't infallible," Linc said. "You expect everything he tells you to do to bring instant results?"

Pete said, "Pull the record on Larry Coons, will you, Julie? He's an offensive fullback, and also a field man. Shot put and discus."

Julie went over to the bank of file cabinets against the left wall, thumbed through one of the drawers and drew out an eight-and-a-half-by-eleven-inch card.

"Lancelot Coons?" she inquired.

Linc said, *"Lancelot!"* and Pete grinned delightedly.

After studying the card, Julie said, "Well, I guess he calls himself Lawrence. He's signed himself Lawrence Coons. But according to this, his legal name is Lancelot."

"In his right arm was the strength of a hundred men because his heart was pure," Linc quoted.

Pete said, "Wonder how many times in his childhood he had that line thrown at him, before he switched to Lawrence. You can hardly blame him for changing it."

Julie, still studying the card, said, "Two years he was all-conference fullback. He holds the school record for the sixteen-pound shot put, and also for the discus throw. He's no world-beater as a scholar, though. He's had a C-minus average for three years." She looked up at Pete. "Want to look over his card yourself?"

Pete shook his head. "I wouldn't know what to look for. We just wanted some general information about him."

"Knowing his real name may pay off," Linc said, grinning. "If we run out of spending money, that ought to be good for a few bucks in blackmail."

Julie put the card away and returned to her desk. "Are you two all registered?" she asked.

"Uh-huh," Pete said. "We haven't a thing to do until

our first classes at nine tomorrow morning. Can we take you to lunch?"

Julie gave her head a regretful shake. "I have a luncheon date."

"Oh? Anybody we know?"

"Somebody you're going to, because he looked over your forged records with considerable interest. He's the track coach."

Linc said, "Professor Kuehn?"

"You already know him?" Julie asked with raised brows.

Linc shook his head. "Just his name. We're both in his class in medieval history."

"Well, you'll also hear from him as track coach. All the coaches have been in to search the files for promising athletes, and Barney was quite interested in you two."

"Barney?" Pete said with a frown. "You're on a first-name basis with the professor?"

"Of course. He's taken me to lunch several times, and twice to dinner. As a matter of fact, I have another dinner date with him tonight."

Pete said indignantly, "Why do you want to run around with an old man?"

Julie laughed. "Professors aren't all fossils, Pete. This one happens to be twenty-seven years old."

"Oh," Pete said, making a mental adjustment. Then he said rather lamely, "That's still pretty old for you."

Julie examined him curiously. There had never been any suggestion of romantic interest on Pete's part for her, yet he often exhibited mild jealousy over the men she became involved with in the line of duty. As fond as she was of Pete, Julie had no romantic feeling for him either, but she was too feminine not to feel secret delight instead of resentment at Pete's occasional jealousies.

Pete half expected to be told to mind his own business, but she surprised him by saying, "I thought it might be helpful to have an inside line with the track coach."

After considering, Pete said reluctantly, "Well, I guess it might at that."

At that moment, the door opened and a tall, handsome man, with a blond crew cut, strode in. Wearing an Ivy League suit, a white shirt with a button-down collar and a quiet-toned necktie, he looked like some bright, young Madison Avenue executive.

He said, "Ready, Julie?" then glanced curiously at Pete and Linc.

Julie said, "This is Pete Cochrane and Linc Hayes, Professor. Professor Kuehn, boys."

The track-coach-history-professor offered each a firm handclasp and a flashing white smile.

"You're the two new transferees from Central College in Missouri, aren't you?" he asked.

When both boys said they were, Kuehn said, "I've gone over your records, and we can certainly use you, when the track season starts. You both plan to come out, I hope."

Linc nodded, and Pete said, "Yes, sir, of course. When do you usually start training around here?"

"We won't get into real training or have tryouts even for indoor track for a couple of months yet. But around the first of October, I usually start everyone on conditioning and limbering up exercises in the field house. There will be announcements in the school paper and on the various bulletin boards."

"We'll watch for them," Pete said. "We're also both in your class in medieval history, Professor."

"Oh? Fine. Then I'll see you both tomorrow morning." He turned back to Julie. "Ready?"

"As soon as I see if Mr. Doyle wants anything before I leave," she said, pressing a switch on her desk intercom. Into it she said, "I'm leaving for lunch now, sir. Do you need anything before I go?"

Mark Doyle's voice replied, "No, go ahead, Julie."

Pete and Linc left the office with Julie and Professor Kuehn, but parted with them outside the building. The professor had a flashy, little red sports car parked in front of the Athletic Administration Building in the drive circling it, which was clearly posted for no parking.

"I'd drop you boys somewhere, but my car's only a two-seater," the professor apologized.

He helped Julie into the car, climbed under the

wheel and roared off as though he were driving a midget racer.

Since they couldn't take Julie to lunch, Pete and Linc decided to eat at the men's dormitory. Lunch was served in the dining hall at twelve fifteen and they just made it. Afterward they went up to their room.

Both bathroom doors were open when they let themselves in. Pete, with Linc trailing after him, walked through the bathroom and peered into the other room. Scooter Miller, alone in the room, was on his bed with a pillow behind his back, reading a magazine.

"Hi, fellows," he said, closing the magazine and tossing it onto the foot of the bed. "Come on in."

Pete went over and sat on the far bed. Linc moved into the room behind Pete, pulled the straight-backed chair away from the writing desk on Scooter's side of the room, spun it around and straddled it, resting his forearms on its back.

Pete asked, "Where's Larry?"

"Football skull session," the track star said. "Coach Blount doesn't waste any time putting his players to work. That's why we keep taking conference championships. You guys get all registered?"

"Uh-huh," Pete said. "One course we're both taking is medieval history under Professor Kuehn. We met him just before lunch. Seems like a nice guy."

"The coach? He is. You'll get a little fed up with him when the track season starts, though. He's a slave driver."

Linc said, "A good coach almost has to be."

"Sure. I'm not complaining about him. I'm just warning you what to expect. You'll work out until you could run from here to San Diego without getting winded."

"If we go out for track," Pete said.

Scooter Miller gave him an astonished look. "If? With the records you guys hold, you have to."

"Depends on how much time our jobs allow us," Pete said.

"What jobs?"

"Well, we don't have any yet, but we're going to have to find a couple. Neither of us get any financial help from our parents, and we're in school on shoestrings. After-school jobs take precedence over track and field."

Miller made a dismissing gesture. "Student Placement Service will find you jobs with hours that won't interfere with training. Athletes get first crack at the best jobs. How much money you going to need?"

Pete said, "We earned enough this summer to get through the first semester. Our tuition and fees and our board and room are paid until February. And we have enough reserve for books, spending money and miscellaneous expenses. But we have to earn enough to carry us next semester."

Scooter Miller looked thoughtful. "I might be able to steer you into a few easy bucks, if you're not too particular how you make them," he said.

Linc asked, "How?"

"Oh, I have some connections," Scooter said vaguely. "How particular are you guys about how you make money?"

Neither Pete nor Linc immediately answered, preferring to consider this provocative question from all angles first. Finally Pete said, "If you have in mind something like peddling pot to students, no thanks. It's not moral scruples, but they put you in San Quentin for that."

Miller laughed. "I didn't have anything that illegal in mind. How are your moral scruples if you can pick up a nice sum without getting in trouble?"

Pete looked at Linc, who grinned. "I don't even insist it be legal, so long as it's safe," the black youth said. "I grew up in a dog-eat-dog environment where you took what you could get any way you could get it."

"That's the only kind of environment there is," Pete said dryly. "You think the rules are different in Beverly Hills? They cut your throat more politely there than they do in Watts, probably, but the knife is just as sharp."

"You from Beverly Hills?" Scooter asked in surprise.

"A long time ago," Pete said in a curt tone. "I got myself kicked out of the house some years back."

His tone didn't invite further prying, which is probably why Scooter failed to inquire what had sent him from Beverly Hills to a school in Missouri.

CHAPTER 9

LINC said, "What's this deal you have in mind, Scooter?"

The track star looked speculatively from one to the other. "Let's talk a little more about moral philosophy first. For instance, how's your school spirit?"

The other two gazed at him blankly. Presently Linc said, "Come again?"

"When you guys compete in sports, do you really give it the old college try? Are you willing to do or die for your beloved school?"

Pete snickered. "Aren't you getting a little corny, Scooter? That kind of stuff went out of style along with patriotism."

Linc said, "I think you're missing the point, buddy. I think he's asking if our loyalty to our new Alma Mater would make us draw a line."

Pete threw an inquiring look at Scooter, who nodded and said, "Linc caught."

Pete shrugged. "I never thought about it much, but I guess school to me is just a place to get an education. I don't get a lump in my throat when they sing the school song. As for doing or dying for old Baldwin Hills, I enjoy jumping, but I won't wring my hands in mental agony, if some joker from another school outjumps me."

Linc said, "If I had any school loyalty, I think it would be to Central College. This place is just a collection of buildings, so far as I'm concerned. What you getting at, Scooter?"

Miller again examined both with pursed lips before saying, "Linc, if somebody paid you enough, would you run the hundred in 9.8 or 9.9 instead of in 9.6?"

Linc let a slow grin form on his face. "That's what I figured you were working up to. You've got an arrangement with some bookie, huh?"

"I'm asking the questions," Scooter said in a definite tone.

"Okay," Linc said agreeably. "For enough money I'd run it in 11. Or try for 9 flat."

Pete said, "Count me in, too. For a payoff, I'd be willing to tip the bar at three feet on the high jump or stumble and keep my long jump below twenty."

Scooter gave a satisfied nod. "Keep your mouths shut about this conversation, and I'll see what I can line up for you."

"Who do you have an arrangement with?" Pete inquired.

"Never mind," the track star said in the same definite tone as before. "You don't get to know anything at all, until I've cleared you with him. You'll hear from me in a few days. Meantime, we don't talk about it anymore. If you start bugging me with questions, you'll begin to shape up as bad security risks."

"You don't have to worry about that," Linc said. "We're a pair of clams."

"Yeah," Pete said. "We won't bug you. But if this thing works out, do we have to wait until track season starts to make any money? The second semester will be along by then."

"Oh, I might be able to get you some kind of retainer. I'll let you know."

They left it at that. Scooter Miller changed the subject by asking if he and his roommate had awakened Pete and Linc, when they came in at 1 A.M. the night before. Both boys said they hadn't heard them.

After a few more minutes of desultory conversation, Pete and Linc made an excuse to leave. Pete immediately led the way downstairs and phoned Captain Greer from one of the phone booths in the dormitory lobby. Linc crowded into the booth, too, so that he could listen in, and Pete held the phone so that he could also hear the captain's end of the conversation.

When he got the captain on the phone, Pete said, "We've got a nibble, Captain. Scooter Miller just felt us out concerning how we'd feel about earning some money by throwing track and field events. He must get some kind of bonus for recruiting."

"Probably," Captain Greer said. "Did he mention Eddie Kye?"

"No, but he said he had to clear us with whoever he deals with, and presumably that's Kye. He warned us not to bug him with any questions or he'd have to consider us security risks."

"Then don't bug him," the captain said. "Just wait for him to come back to you."

"Yes, sir," Pete said. "We'll check back when we get something else to report."

When they emerged from the booth, Linc said, "Now what?"

"I guess we just go through the motions of being students, until Scooter gets back to us."

"Well, maybe we'll learn something," Linc said philosophically.

That evening, Barney Kuehn took Julie to dinner at the Brown Derby. Over coffee, he casually asked her how she happened to know Pete Cochrane and Linc Hayes.

Aware that their school records stuck pretty close to the truth, except for their mythical two years at Central College, Julie thought it was safe enough to say, "They're both originally from this area. I met them at a high-school dance long ago."

"How well do you know them?"

"Well, I consider them friends," Julie said cautiously. "Why?"

"Do you know much about them?"

Julie decided that if she admitted she did, he might ask some questions about the boys that she would find it awkward to answer. She temporized by saying, "About their backgrounds? Not really, except what I read in their school records."

"Did you have any contact with them while they were away at school in Missouri?" he asked. "I mean did you correspond?"

Wondering what he was getting at, Julie said warily, "No, we aren't that close friends." She was operating on the principle that it is safest to stick to the truth as much as possible on unimportant details, when you are trying to get a lie across.

"Were you aware they were away at school? I mean before they showed up at Baldwin Hills."

Julie started to shake her head, then changed her mind and said, "Well, I saw their records before I saw them. As a matter of fact, I gave them to you along with those of all the other potential track men."

"But prior to that you'd been out of contact with them for a long time?" he persisted. "You hadn't even heard from mutual friends that they were away at school?"

For some reason he suspected their records were forged, she thought with dismay. Now she wished she had claimed a more intimate relationship with Pete and Linc, so that she could allay his suspicions by asserting positive knowledge of their attendance at the Missouri school, but it was too late for that. All she could do was play it out the way she had started.

"No," she said. "But why are you asking me all these questions, Barney? You sound as though you suspect them of some kind of wrongdoing."

"Not really," he said. "Just a peculiar thought I had which is probably a pipe dream. Don't worry your little head about it."

But she did worry about it, enough to make her place a call for Pete at the men's dorm, when she got home at about 11:30 P.M. The boy who answered the second-floor phone returned after going to see if Pete was in, to announce that he and his roommate were both out on dates.

Before she left for work the next morning, Julie phoned again and this time got hold of Pete. She asked him and Linc to stop by her office, when they got a chance.

As neither had ten o'clock classes on Wednesdays, they stopped by to see her then. No one was in the outer office, when they arrived. They found Julie taking dictation in Mark Doyle's private office. The athletic director told them to come in and close the door, so that they could confer in privacy.

Julie had already told Mark Doyle about the searching questions Barney Kuehn had asked her the night before. She repeated the story for the benefit of Pete and Linc.

When she finished, Pete said with a frown, "Sounds to me like he suspects we're in school on faked records." He looked at Doyle. "Could he have spotted them as fake?"

"I don't see how," the athletic director said. "We did a pretty thorough job of forgery."

"Maybe we ran into him somewhere on some other case," Linc hazarded. "Maybe he remembers we were cops."

"No, I'm sure it's nothing that definite," Julie said. "And I'm certain he hasn't the slightest suspicion that I'm a cop."

"What's bugging him, then?" Linc asked.

Julie said, "I got the impression he didn't have any specific suspicion, but for some reason he just thinks there is something fishy about you two. What made him think that, I couldn't say."

Doyle said puzzledly, "He discussed both you boys' track and field records with me, and he didn't indicate any suspicion then. Of course, that was several days ago, just after I'd had Julie plant your records in the files."

Pete shrugged. "There isn't anything we can do about it, so why worry? If he makes any actual accusations about us not being bona fide students, he'll probably come to you first, won't he, Mr. Doyle?"

"Probably," Doyle agreed.

"In that case, I guess all you could do is take him into your confidence. Meanwhile, let's just sit on it."

Julie said, "I don't understand why the college president wants this thing kept from the coaches, anyway. They might be a help."

Mark Doyle cleared his throat before saying with some reluctance, "Dr. Vester is taking into consideration the possibility that one or more of the coaches may be involved in the matter. It is a possibility, of course, although personally I consider it rather remote."

"Barney Kuehn couldn't possibly be connected with this racket," Julie said with indignation.

All three males looked at her. Julie blushed.

"You getting a little emotionally involved in this case?" Pete inquired sardonically. "Remember what they told us at Police Academy about emotional involvement with suspects."

"I'm just making a character judgment," Julie said primly. "That doesn't mean I'm emotionally involved. Besides, Barney Kuehn is not a suspect!"

CHAPTER 10

PETE and Linc got through their first day of classes without incident. That evening after dinner, Dewey Stockton and his skinny roommate dropped by their room.

As the goateed black youth closed the door from the hall behind them, Arnie Trotter glanced toward the bathroom and saw that both connecting doors stood open. He walked through the bathroom to close the door into Miller's and Coons' room, then carefully closed the other one also when he came back into Pete and Linc's room.

Pete was seated on his bed in stocking feet, a pillow propped behind his back, reading his medieval history assignment. Linc was doing the same thing at his writing desk.

Pete closed his book, dropped it alongside of him on the bed and examined the visitors curiously. Linc swung around to straddle the straight-backed chair he was seated in and examined them with equal curiosity.

"Why the cloak-and-dagger manner?" Pete inquired.

The satanic-looking Dewey Stockton went over to sit on Linc's bed. The long-haired white boy with the Fu Manchu moustache took the other straight-backed chair.

Stockton said, "Are you guys in sympathy with the aims of the Afro-American Student Union?"

Linc said, "Depends on what they are, pal."
Stockton frowned at him. "I figured you in automatically, Linc, being a soul brother. Mainly I was talking to your roommate."
"Well, talk to me, too. I don't let anybody do my thinking for me, even soul brothers."
"You'll go along," Stockton said with confidence. "Every demand we're going to make is for something long overdue. What we want, though, is not just your sympathy but your active participation tomorrow."
"Participation in what?" Pete asked.
"We're going to take over the administration building and occupy it until all our demands are met."
Pete and Linc looked at each other, then back at the president of the Afro-American Student Union.
Linc said, "What are your demands?"
"Well, first we want a department of Afro-American studies established."
"I'll go along with that," Linc said. "Every school ought to have one."
"Second, we want sole right to choose its instructors."
Linc cocked an eyebrow at him. "From qualified personnel, I hope."
"Of course, but by our rules of qualification, not the school administration's. We don't want black Ph.D.s who grew up in white middle-class neighborhoods. We want instructors who can tell it like it is, even if they have no formal education at all."
Pete said, "Black militants, you mean."
"I don't like that term," Dewey told him. "Let's say men who have pulled themselves out of the ghetto, but still remember enough of what it was like to have something meaningful to say. They'd be educated men, but not necessarily with formal educations. They'd be picked for their knowledge, not their degrees."
Linc said, "I didn't know you had a degree in educational administration, Dewey."
The bearded black youth gave him a startled look. "What?"
"Well, now, you've decided that you're better qualified to choose the instructors for this school than Dr. Vester, who does hold an advanced degree in educa-

tional administration. So I assume you have credentials to offer to balance his."

Dewey Stockton looked disgusted. "What are you, an Uncle Tom?"

Linc smiled from the teeth out. "I'm probably just as militant as you are, buddy. I even used to riot down in Watts over the injustices inflicted on our race. But I don't remember you being extrabright in high school. Why the devil should I trust your judgment over Dr. Vester's about who's going to instruct me?"

"It wouldn't be my judgment," Stockton said irritably. "The whole Afro-American Student Union would have to agree on who was to be hired. You'd have as much say as I would."

"I don't think these guys see things our way, Dewey," the long-haired Arnie Trotter said. "I think this is a mistake."

"So far I'm fifty percent with you," Linc told him, then turned back to the other black youth. "Go on with your other demands, Dewey. I won't interrupt again until you've listed them all."

"Okay," Dewey said. "We want one floor of one wing of the men's dormitory reserved for black students only, and we want a separate black lounge in the Student Union. We want a separate section of the dining hall set aside for blacks, with a separate menu of soul food. We want all black applicants, who are approved by the Afro-American Student Union for admission to the school to be accepted, regardless of educational qualifications. And we want a guarantee that no disciplinary action will be taken against any of the students who occupy Rogers Memorial Hall tomorrow."

When he stopped speaking, Linc said, "That's it?"

"For this round. We have a few future demands in mind."

Linc looked over at Pete. "You have any comments before I start, buddy-boy?"

Pete said to Arnie Trotter, "Is the Students for a Democratic Society backing this move?"

"All the way," Trotter said.

"You don't like rooming with Dewey, huh?"

Trotter emitted a bored sigh, as though this was a

cliché he had heard over and over from members of the Establishment.

"Well, you must not, or you wouldn't be supporting this separatist movement," Pete said reasonably. "They're not going to let you in that black section of the dorm."

Linc said, "Dewey's the one asking for a separate black section, so it sounds more like he doesn't like rooming with Trotter."

Arnie Trotter said in a digusted tone, "That's a typical square argument, Hayes. The principle involved supercedes any personal feelings. Dewey and I are close friends, but if we have to split up in order to accomplish a worthwhile aim, we're willing to do it. Reforms seldom come without some sacrifice."

"You're not interested in reform," Pete said. "You've attached yourself to this movement just as an excuse to agitate and give the school administrators another headache. Your organization has made it pretty clear that your ultimate goal is anarchy, and your first step is to attempt to destroy the colleges and universities. You don't give a hoot in Hades about the principles involved here. You simply want to shut this college down."

"That's not true," Trotter denied hotly. "You must have gotten your picture of the SDS from *Time* magazine. Why would I want to shut down the school when I'm paying tuition to attend?"

"The ultimate aim of the SDS isn't anarchy?" Pete demanded.

"Our ultimate goal is to tear down the present corrupt Establishment and rebuild American society from scratch," Trotter said. "Maybe you call that anarchy, but I call it a search for true democracy. We don't have any in our present society."

"There's plenty wrong with our society," Pete conceded. "But what's wrong with trying to mend it from within, instead of flushing the good parts down the drain along with the bad?"

"It's beyond mending. The powers that be are too firmly entrenched. And there aren't any good parts. The only solution is to uproot the whole system and start over."

Linc said, "You figure when that happens, the good guys will take over, huh?"

"What's that supposed to mean?"

"What makes you think another set of bad guys, maybe even worse than the present Establishment, won't end up in the saddle? By historical precedent, the odds are that they will."

Trotter said, "No system built on the ashes of the present one could be worse than what we now have in America."

"You haven't read much history, pal," Linc told him. "When the French Revolution destroyed the Establishment in France, they eventually ended up with Napoleon. When the Russians destroyed their Establishment in 1917, they eventually ended up with Stalin. Then there was Hitler and Mussolini, just to mention a couple of other results of Establishments being uprooted."

"Sure, use the right-wing techniques of picking all the bad examples," Trotter said scornfully. "Why don't you mention Mao Tse-tung, Ho Chi Minh or Fidel Castro?"

Pete and Linc both looked at him blankly, then at each other. Pete said, "Is he citing them as *good* examples?"

"I think so," Linc said, suddenly grinning with amusement. "Which makes me pass any further argument. I can't argue with this guy any more, because we don't speak the same language."

"I was about to make the same observation," Trotter said.

Dewey Stockton said irritably, "If you characters are finished with your political discussion, let's get back to the original subject. Linc, are you and Pete in or not?"

"I'm not," Linc said in a definite tone. "I can't back any of your demands, Dewey, except for an Afro-American studies course. I was too long getting out of the ghetto to want to move back into another one here. I happen to like rooming with Pete."

"That's incidental," the bearded black youth said with increased irritation. "You miss the whole point, Linc."

Linc shrugged. "I listened to you carefully. I must have missed the point about the school being required to admit all black applicants regardless of educational qualifications, too. If standards are going to be lowered for us, why not for whites, too?"

"Because blacks haven't had a chance to acquire the necessary educational qualifications, while whites have had. It's that simple."

Linc made a dismissing gesture. "I won't push my objection to that too much, because it's true that blacks don't get as good a public school education as whites for a number of sociological and psychological reasons. But I think the problem could better be attacked some other way. But let's consider your demand for soul food in the dining hall. I ate all the chitlings and pigs' feet and ham hocks I ever intend to when I was poor. You must know that most soul-food recipes came from attempts to make palatable the scraps of food sent down to slave quarters because they weren't fit to be served in the big house. I'll take steak and potatoes, thanks. As for your last demand, Martin Luther King never asked for amnesty, and he was the guy who started all this."

Dewey gave his head a morose shake and said, "Boy, I never thought I'd see Linc Hayes develop into an Uncle Tom."

In an exasperated voice Linc said, "I never thought I'd see Dewey Stockton develop into a bigot."

"A bigot!" Dewey said on a high note.

"You want to keep whites out of your neighborhood, don't you? What else can you call it?"

"Oh Linc, Linc," Dewey said with the forced patience of a parent explaining something to a child. "The separatist movement is merely recognition that Whitey doesn't want us in his society. I'd be quite willing to enter what sociologists keep calling the mainstream of American life, if Whitey would let me, but he won't. I know there's a few white guys, like Arnie and Pete, who really don't care that we're black, but the majority hasn't changed a bit. Just try buying a house in Beverly Hills."

Linc said, "I'm aware that bigotry isn't dead, Dewey. A lot of whites will never change their old, narrow attitudes. But the important thing is that *I've* changed. When I was a kid, white clerks in the stores used to call me 'boy,' and I took it, even though I resented it. I don't suppose many of those clerks have changed their mental attitudes, but none of them condescend to me anymore just because I'm black. You know why?"

"Okay, why?"

Linc spaced his words slowly and definitely. "Because they know I'll no longer take it. Maybe inside of him a white clerk who waits on me is secretly thinking of me as a nigger, but he's not about to show it these days. He's going to call me 'sir' and be just as polite as he is to white customers. This isn't because of any mass change in social attitudes. It's because of a massive change in me. I've gained enough self-respect to look any white man straight in the eye, no longer just wistfully wishing I was as good as him, but being absolutely certain I'm at least as good, and maybe better, if he's stupid enough to be a bigot. Probably prejudiced whites don't even know the real reason they no longer try to push me around, but I know. It's because my old sense of inferiority is gone forever, and it's been replaced by a hard core of pride that they can almost see and don't dare test. I don't care what whites think about me. What's important is what I think about me. I consider that the biggest gain I've gotten out of the civil rights movement."

When he stopped speaking, Pete brought his palms together in a silent pantomime of applause. "Bravo. I didn't know you were such an orator, Linc."

Linc looked a trifle sheepish. "Guess I got a little carried away. But I think blacks are making progress toward real equality, even if we are still only halfway there. And I won't be party to reversing what progress we've already made. So count me out for your demonstration, Dewey."

"Me too," Pete said. "I go along with Linc."

With a shrug, Dewey Stockton rose to his feet. "I guess that's that. Can we at least count on you not to tip off the school authorities?"

Linc gave him an aggrieved look, and Dewey had the

grace to look abashed. "Sorry," he said. "I know that was an unnecessary question."

Arnie Trotter cocked his head as though listening. Suddenly, he rose to his feet and tiptoed to the bathroom door, which was only a few feet from where he sat. Grasping the knob, he abruptly jerked open the door.

Scooter Miller nearly fell into the room. Recovering his balance, he assumed a false smile, said, "Hi, fellows," retreated into his own room and closed the door behind him.

Scowling at the closed door, Dewey said, "Wonder how much he heard?"

"Probably not about your plans to take over Roger Memorial Hall," Linc reassured him. "I don't think that's been mentioned since right after you got here, has it?"

He glanced around at the others, but no one was really sure.

"If he finks to the administration, he's going to be in trouble," Dewey said savagely. "I've been thinking of tangling with that guy for some time."

CHAPTER 11

THURSDAY morning, Pete and Linc both had classes in the liberal arts building. When they reached the quadrangle at about a quarter of nine, they found it crammed with students. The mob was faced toward the administration building, and those in the foreground were steadily chanting, "Pigs, pigs, pigs!"

Art Feister, the six-foot-seven-inch basketball player who lived directly across the hall from Pete and Linc, was standing on the outer fringe of the crowd with his Mexican-American roommate, Cesar Ramirez. Pete and Linc stopped next to them to inquire what was going on.

"Some bunch of radical students tried to take over the administration building," the lanky Feister informed them. "They found it full of cops."

Pete and Linc looked at each other. Pete said, "Wonder if we'll be blamed?"

Linc shook his head. "Dewey will know it wasn't us."

Dewey Stockton, elbowing his way from the vanguard of the crowd to the rear, emerged near where the four stood. Spotting Pete and Linc, he came over.

In a furious voice he said to Linc, "Scooter did overhear our plans last night. They've got the place staked out with enough cops to hold off a regiment."

Linc said, "You can't be sure it was Scooter who finked."

"Was it you or Pete?" the goateed black youth demanded.

"You know better than that," Linc said reproachfully.

"Then it had to be Scooter," Dewey snapped. "Nobody else outside the members of the AASU or the SDS knew anything about it."

Cesar Ramirez said, "You talking about Scooter Miller, Dewey?"

Apparently the Mexican-American and his skyscraper roommate were regarded as members of the Establishment by Dewey Stockton. Up to now, he hadn't even acknowledged their presence, and his reply to the question was hardly cordial.

"That's right," he said frigidly. "When you see your pal, tell him he'd better start looking over his shoulder, because I'm going to get even for this."

He strode off angrily as the other four students stared after him. Art Feister said, "What was he talking about, anyway?"

Pete said, "We'll fill you in later. Linc and I have nine o'clock classes."

He and Linc moved on around the edge of the crowd to the liberal arts building.

When they emerged from their classes an hour later, the crowd had dispersed. Later they learned that Dr. Duane Vester, the college president, had appeared to announce that he would tolerate no violence of any kind by student protesters, but was willing to meet with a delegation from the Afro-American Student Union to consider all their demands. Since Dewey Stockton, the leader of the black agitators, had already disappeared from the scene in disgust, the rest of the AASU members and their supporting Students for a Democratic Society members apparently decided there was no point in further demonstration, and retired to consider Dr. Vester's proposal.

There were no further student demonstrations that week. Pete and Linc attended the rest of their Thursday classes and their Friday classes without incident, and began to adjust to college life. Friday evening, they went on a double date with Eve Evans and Althea Moore.

In line with their roles as students who had to watch their pennies, they offered the girls a rather modest evening. They took them to a movie, then to the Petöfi Club.

While Linc and Althea were over at the jukebox choosing numbers, Pete casually mentioned to Eve that he might be in a position to show her a better time before long.

"Have you lined up a job?" she inquired.

Pete shook his head. "I just have a deal pending. Linc, too. Your ex-boyfriend is arranging it."

Eve glanced at him sharply. "Scooter?"

"Do I know any other ex-boyfriends of yours?" he inquired with raised brows.

Eve looked upset. "Does this deal involve a man named Eddie Kye?"

Pete shrugged. "Scooter never mentioned him."

"Does it involve gamblers?" she persisted. "Are they . . . are you being offered money not to do as well as you can when the track season starts?"

Pete frowned at her. "Hey, what do you know about this?"

"Enough to know you can get in deep trouble, if you let Scooter line up any deals for you," the girl said urgently. "Pete, the school authorities know about this and are secretly investigating the athletes involved. You could get yourself expelled."

"How do you know there's an investigation going on?" Pete asked, letting his frown deepen.

Eve blinked, momentarily stymied for an answer. But she immediately demonstrated a talent for thinking on her feet, because her hesitation lasted no more than a second. "Have you met Mr. Doyle's new secretary?" she inquired.

"Julie Barnes?" Pete asked, surprised. "Uh-huh."

"We're friends," Eve said "She told me about it in confidence."

Pete managed to keep his amusement at this bald-faced lie from showing on his face. Obviously, Eve had dredged up this explanation for her inside knowledge, because she didn't care to admit informing on her ex-boyfriend.

He said, "How much did Julie tell you?"

"Just that they think some gambler named Eddie Kye is bribing Baldwin Hills athletes. How they found out, or who the athletes are other than Scooter, I couldn't say. She only told me about this because she knew I used to go with him, and she thought I'd be interested." After a pause she said, "I wasn't, really. At least, I wasn't concerned."

"Did Scooter ever admit taking any bribes to you?"

"No," she lied. "All I know about it is what Julie told me."

It seemed apparent she was going to stick to that story, so as to avoid having to answer more questions. Pete could see no point in probing further.

Eve said, "Incidentally, Julie told me this in strict confidence. You won't mention anything about it to her, will you?"

"Of course not."

"And you won't tip off Scooter, will you?"

"Not if you ask me not to."

"Then I'm asking you," she said, relieved. "I have one more request, Pete. Don't get involved in this."

He smiled at her. "After your warning? I have no desire to get myself expelled."

Eve looked even more relieved. "Don't let Linc get involved either, will you? But don't mention it in front of Althea. She doesn't know anything about it."

"All right," Pete agreed.

They dropped the subject then, because Linc and Althea returned to the booth.

There were no further developments on the case over that weekend. But on Monday afternoon an incident of some significance occurred.

Pete and Linc were descending the stairs from the second floor of the dormitory, when a short, stocky, balding man of about thirty in a greenish-gray uniform entered the building, carrying about a dozen pieces of clothing on hangers and in individual plastic bags. He heaved them onto the counter, and the student clerk on duty pulled them across to hang them on a metal rod.

"That's all the cleaning this trip," the man said. "The laundry will take me a couple of trips."

Pete and Linc reached the bottom of the stairs, as the man went out again. The clerk on duty was the same lanky youth who had been there when they checked in on Labor Day. They had since learned that his name was Luke Small, and that, despite his youthful appearance, he was a senior. They paused to speak to him.

Pete said, "I didn't know we had cleaning and laundry delivery service."

"You should read the bulletin board," Luke said. "Pickups are Monday and Thursday afternoons. Monday's stuff comes back on Thursday, Thursday's stuff the following Monday."

The stocky man came back in, carrying a huge pile of laundry bundles. The clerk stowed them under the counter. As the delivery man went outside for another load, Pete idly noted that the lettering on the back of his uniform read *Cord Laundry and Cleaning Co.*

"That Cord himself?" he asked Luke Small.

The clerk shook his head. "I don't even know if there is a guy named Cord. Maybe it's just a company name. This guy is Johnny Merlin."

The stocky Johnny Merlin returned with another load of packages. When these too had been stowed away, Luke produced a large manila envelope from beneath the counter and handed it over.

"All the money and slips so far are in here," he said. "There should be lots more bets, so I'll start another envelope for you to pick up Thursday."

"Okay," the stocky man said, and went out carrying the envelope.

Linc said, "Last Monday was Labor Day, so the first pickup that guy made must have been last Thursday. This has to be that pickup coming back, so you haven't collected for any cleaning or laundry so far this year, Luke. That money and slips you mentioned was for something else, huh?"

"Bets on next Saturday's game," the clerk said.

He referred to the first football game of the season, with Moorpark College, Linc surmised. He said, "What is he, a bookie?"

"Johnny?" Luke said. "Naw, just a runner for some bookie."

Pete said, "And you're a runner for him?"

"I stand still," the lanky youth said with a grin. "The guys come to me. You fellows want to place bets?"

Linc said, "What's the spread?"

"Moorpark gets a ten-point spot."

Linc made a face. "My school spirit keeps me from betting on Moorpark, and that spot keeps me from backing Baldwin Hills."

"I'll pass, too," Pete said. "You do much business?"

"Not on this first game, so far. But by the time the season's really underway, I'll be handling a grand a week."

"Just from the men's dorm?" Pete asked in surprise.

"Oh, no. I've got a chick in the girls' dorm taking bets for me, too. Plus a lot of students who don't live in the dorm, at least among the upperclassmen, know where to find me."

Linc said, "How long you been doing this?"

"This is my second year. And my last, of course, because I graduate in June, barring failure."

"This Merlin guy will need a replacement for next year," Linc said hopefully. "Pete and I will still be here."

"Sorry," Luke told him. "I've already picked a sophomore to groom as heir apparent, and I've got him stirring up a little action among the new freshmen."

Linc looked disappointed. Pete said, "Do you catch many bets against Baldwin Hills?"

Luke shook his head. "School spirit, you know. If the guys think Baldwin Hills is going to get clobbered, they tend not to bet at all. But we usually have pretty good teams, so there's normally pretty good action."

"When Baldwin Hills wins, this bookie gets hit pretty bad then, huh?"

"Only if we win by more than the spot. And last year he was luckier than the devil. There were only two football games, one basketball game and a baseball game where he had to pay off."

"That is luck," Pete said. "I'd like to have a piece of this operation."

"No chance," the clerk told him. "But you might make some money betting. The bookie's luck is bound to turn."

Linc said, "You are a funny man, Luke. You never see bookies in bankruptcy court. Only their best customers."

CHAPTER 12

PETE and Linc moved on into the dormitory lobby. A number of students were watching television there. The pair halted beyond hearing range of any of them.

"Think this Johnny Merlin is tied in with Eddie Kye?" Pete asked.

"I would almost bet on it," Linc said. "What a sweet setup. A grand a week in bets rolling in, most of it on Baldwin Hills, and a system to keep down Baldwin Hills' scores."

"And whoever is running this racket could be laying heavy money on Baldwin Hills' opponents with other bookies."

After considering this, Linc nodded. "Of course. He cleans up two ways. Think we better report this development to the captain?"

"Uh-huh," Pete said, and moved over to the line of phone booths against the far wall.

When Pete got the captain on the phone and had made his report, Captain Greer decided it was time for a conference. He told Pete to pick up Julie, when she got off work at five o'clock, and for all three of them to come to his office at six.

"Hate to keep you overtime, Captain," Pete said. "Maybe Julie can get off early."

"I won't be available earlier, because I have other appointments," the captain told him. "Just be here at six."

"Yes, sir," Pete said, and hung up.

"Bad news?" Linc asked when Pete emerged from the booth, after examining his expression.

Pete shook his head. "I just sometimes get irked at the captain's peremptory manner. We're ordered to appear promptly at six. Julie, too."

"Gives us plenty of time," Linc said, glancing at his watch. "It's only three fifteen."

When they picked her up at her office at five, Julie was considerably amused to learn that she was such a close friend of Eve Evans that she confided office secrets in her.

The three of them arrived downtown with forty minutes to spare before the scheduled meeting. Julie suggested they grab an early dinner in the Police Building cafeteria. Linc vetoed the suggestion.

"If the captain keeps us late, maybe his conscience will hurt him enough to offer to buy us all dinner," he said. "Why pass a chance to stick him?"

Pete said, "I had other plans anyway. Let's check out Johnny Merlin at R. and I."

When they gave the clerk on duty at the R. and I. counter the name Johnny Merlin, it developed that he had a record. They went to the Golden Horseshoe, pulled his package and sat at one of the tables.

The suspect was listed as Jonathan (Johnny) Merlin, age thirty-two, and was described as five feet seven inches tall and weighing 185 pounds. He was unmarried, and his address at the time of last contact with the police—nearly two years previously—had been a rooming house on Franklin Avenue in the Hollywood District.

Merlin had a considerably longer record than Eddie Kye. His criminal career had started at the age of fourteen, with an arrest for petty theft. During the next four years he had managed to get himself arrested seven more times for offenses ranging from malicious destruction of property to grand theft, auto. Until he was eighteen, all of his troubles with the law had been handled by juvenile authorities, of course, and despite several convictions, he was never given any sentence other than probation.

Apparently Johnny Merlin either had behaved himself for a time after reaching eighteen or had finally become sly enough to avoid arrest, because there was no further mark on his record until he turned twenty. Then he was arrested for armed robbery of a loan company.

In California a suspect between the ages of eighteen and twenty-one may, at the discretion of the court, either be tried as an adult or handled as a juvenile. Presumably because he hadn't been in trouble for two whole years, the court in this case decided to refer Merlin to the juvenile authorities again. He was placed on probation until his twenty-first birthday.

Two days after reaching twenty-one, Merlin shot and critically wounded a customer during a drugstore robbery. Tried as an adult this time, he was convicted of armed robbery and assault with a deadly weapon, and was given a sentence of from five years to life. He served the full five years and was paroled at the age of twenty-six.

Since his release from San Quentin, Merlin had a total of fourteen arrests on charges ranging from extortion to suspicion of homicide, but he had never again been convicted of anything. Since his graduation from prison, it seemed there were always several witnesses to alibi him for whatever offense he was accused of.

A note in the file from the Intelligence Division made it clear why defense witnesses were always so conveniently available. Johnny Merlin had become part of the organization of racketeer and loan-shark Dinny Cord.

Linc said, "Hey, Eddie Kye was listed as once being a collector for this same Cord guy."

Julie said, "That's right. Maybe we've stumbled on the man who's the brains of this racket."

Pete's eyes suddenly widened. "It just registered on me that Merlin works for the Cord Laundry and Cleaning Company."

Linc looked across at him. "That's right," he said slowly. "Maybe we'd better pull this Dinny Cord's package. I'll go get his D.R. number."

The black youth rose to his feet and headed for the R. and I. counter. When he returned with the proper Division of Records number, he located the manila envelope bearing that number and carried it back to the table.

According to his record, Dinsmore (Dinny) Cord was fifty-four years old. He must have been built like a beanpole, because he was described as six feet one inch tall, but weighed only 135 pounds. He was a widower without children and lived on Rochester Avenue in West Los Angeles, in an area of exclusive and expensive apartment houses. His mug shots showed a thin, cadaverous face with a beaked nose between piercing black eyes. He had a full head of curling hair, described as salt-and-pepper gray.

Dinny Cord had a long list of arrests going back nearly thirty years. Most of them were on suspicion of either assault or extortion, but twice he had been picked up on suspicion of conspiracy to commit murder, and once on a complaint of usury. He had only one conviction, though. At the age of twenty-nine, he had drawn a suspended sentence for simple assault.

"Typical hood," Pete groused. "A million arrests, but he always gets off because he's defended by some high-priced mouthpiece, and a dozen other hoods are willing to commit perjury for him."

"They caught him that once," Julie pointed out.

"Big deal," Pete said disgustedly. "Six-month suspended sentence."

"I don't see anything about him running a cleaning and laundry company," Linc said.

Pete examined the record again. "Maybe it's a recent acquisition," he said presently. "Intelligence Division would know. Let's stop by there."

They left R. and I. and took an elevator to the seventh floor. In the Intelligence Division squad room they glanced around to see if they knew any of the officers on duty.

"There's Ed Forbes," Julie said, pointing to a lean, crew-cut man in a neat business suit, who was working with some papers at a table across the room.

They crossed the room together and halted on the opposite side of the table from the officer Julie had indicated. Pete said, "Hi, Lieutenant."

Lieutenant Edward Forbes glanced up, and his face split in a welcoming grin. "Well, well, the Mod Squad. Sit down." He pushed his papers aside and indicated chairs across the table from him.

The function of the LAPD Intelligence Division was to keep tabs on organized crime and trade data with similar intelligence units in other cities. When Pete, Linc and Julie were settled in chairs, Pete asked the lieutenant for a rundown on the current activities of Dinny Cord.

"I can give you that without even pulling his file," Forbes said. "He's one of my assigned headaches. He's been driving me crazy for the past year and a half."

"How's that?" Linc asked.

"He's been making all the motions of going legit. I'd like to believe him, but I've never yet seen an old-time racketeer who really went straight. I keep thinking he must be pulling something crooked, but I can't figure what."

"Maybe we can help you," Pete said. "By his going legit, are you referring to his being in the laundry and cleaning business?"

Lieutenant Forbes looked surprised. "You know about that?"

"Not as much as we'd like to."

Forbes shrugged. "There isn't much to know. It's a small place on Los Angeles Street, only a few blocks from here. Dinny bought out its former owner about a year and a half ago. We think he's probably still loansharking, but since he went into the laundry and cleaning business, there's been no evidence of him continuing his old periodic racket of extorting protection money from small merchants. Maybe because he's a small merchant himself, now."

Linc grinned at him. "We've got news for you, man. The cleaning and laundry business is just a front for a much safer and more profitable business than the protection racket."

The lieutenant emitted a sigh. "I knew his supposed reform was too good to be true. What's he up to?"

"He's making book on college sports events," Linc said. "And coppering his bets by fixing the games. His delivery man is also his runner for the handbook."

"Now I'll be able to sleep nights," Forbes said with a grin. "I won't have to lie awake fretting about is-he-or-isn't-he still a hood. Give me the details."

Pete glanced at Linc, who said, "Go ahead, you're a good reporter."

Pete explained the case the Mod Squad was working on and described what they had so far learned. He concluded with the same suggestion he had previously made to Linc that the racketeer was probably increasing his take by betting with local bookies on the fixed games. This brought an interested light to Ed Forbes' eyes.

"If Dinny is doing that, the division may have one less hood to worry about before long," the lieutenant said.

Julie asked, "Why do you say that?"

"Dinny's an independent racketeer, with no Mafia connections. Up to now he's always confined himself to loan-sharking and extortion, carefully staying away from gambling rackets. Not because he's unaware of the potential profits in gambling, but because the gambling rackets are controlled by the Cosa Nostra, and outside competition too often ends up dead. Since he's not taking horse bets, the Mafia probably wouldn't care about this college game racket he's apparently running. But if he's fixing games to beat local bookies, he's playing Russian roulette. The Mafia controls local bookies, so if Dinny is taking them, he's taking the Mafia, too. And that can be fatal."

Pete said, "After reading his record, it couldn't happen to a nicer guy."

It was ten of six when Pete, Linc and Julie left the Intelligence squadroom. They headed for Captain Greer's office.

The meeting in the captain's office wasn't very long. Julie and Linc let Pete be the spokesman in reporting everything they had learned so far, including what Lieutenant Forbes had told them, and Pete kept it as brief as possible.

When he finished his report, the captain pursed his lips thoughtfully and said, "It seems pretty evident that this Dinny Cord is the brains behind this racket, but you'll need proof. Scooter Miller hasn't come back to you yet about the deal he was going to arrange, I take it."

"No, sir," Pete said. "Want us to prod him?"

"No," the captain decided. "Not yet, anyway. There's less chance of arousing suspicion if you let him come to you."

Linc said, "Want us to do anything at all?"

"Just stand by until you get bribe offers."

"How about me?" Julie asked. "I don't seem to be accomplishing much."

"Something may develop," the captain told her. "Just continue as Mark Doyle's secretary. Don't get impatient. By now you should know that ninety percent of police undercover work is simply waiting." He glanced around the circle of faces. "Have you kids had dinner?"

They all shook their heads. "That an invitation?" Pete inquired.

"Yeah, I'll pop, if you'll settle for the eighth-floor cafeteria. I haven't time go to anywhere else, because I have a lot of desk work to do after dinner."

Linc threw Julie an I-told-you-so grin, then said to the captain, "We don't look gift horses in the mouths. We accept."

CHAPTER 13

LATE Tuesday afternoon, Pete and Linc were studying at their respective writing desks, when Scooter Miller appeared in the bathroom doorway.

"You guys got a minute?" the handsome track star asked.

Linc glanced over his shoulder, then shifted his chair around to face that way. From his position Pete merely had to turn his head to the right. Both looked at Scooter inquiringly.

"Sure," Pete said. "What's up?"

Leaning against the bathroom doorjamb, Scooter said, "You still interested in that proposition I mentioned?"

Pete said, "As much as ever," and Linc said, "We've been exercising restraint not to bug you about it."

"Okay. I've got a meeting set up for you tonight."

"With who?" Pete asked.

"With a fellow named Eddie Kye. He'll be in a place called Bertie's Bar and Grill at Ninth and Figueroa at 9 P.M. Just introduce yourselves, and he'll take it from there."

"Eddie Kye," Pete repeated, as though memorizing an unfamiliar name. "Bertie's Bar and Grill at Ninth and Figueroa. How do we recognize this guy?"

"He's around forty, not very tall, but must weigh over two-hundred pounds. And not much of it is fat. He's a pretty husky character. He's also a very sharp dresser. He says there's never much business at Bertie's on a Tuesday night, so you shouldn't have any trouble picking him out. Anyway, I described you guys to him, too."

"We'll be there," Linc said. "What did you tell him about us, aside from what we look like?"

"Just what your track and field records were, and that you were both willing to play ball for some easy money."

Linc nodded approval, and Pete said, "Thanks for setting things up, Scooter."

"It wasn't entirely friendship," the track star said with a grin. "I get a bonus for steering you to Eddie. I'll let you get back to your homework."

He disappeared back into his own room.

A couple of minutes before nine that night, Pete and Linc arrived at Ninth and Figueroa Streets in the Woody. At that time of night, there was no parking problem in this area. Pete found a place behind a shiny new Ford almost in front of the tavern on its Figueroa Street side.

Bertie's Bar and Grill was an ordinary neighborhood tavern, with a bar running the length of the left wall and with booths arranged along the right wall. At the rear was a jukebox, a cigarette machine and a pair of rest-room doors.

A beefy bartender, wearing a not-quite-clean apron, was behind the bar. None of the booths were occupied and only four customers were at the bar. Near the door a couple in their thirties sat together. Halfway along was an elderly man in a threadbare suit. At the far end of the bar, in a blue pin-striped suit that must have cost three hundred dollars, Eddie Kye was nursing a draft beer in a handled glass mug.

After glancing around, Pete said in a low voice, "I guess we don't have to pretend we're having trouble figuring which one is him."

He led the way the length of the bar to its far end and said, "Mr. Kye?"

The burly Kye gave him a benign smile. "Uh-huh. You Pete Cochrane?"

"Yes, sir," Pete said. "And this is my buddy, Linc Hayes."

As he shook hands with both of them, Eddie Kye said, "You kids don't have to be formal. I'm not Mr. Kye or Sir. Just call me Eddie."

Linc nodded agreeably, and Pete said, "Okay, Eddie."

"You kids old enough to drink?"

Both avoided direct answer by saying they would have Cokes. The bartender poured two glasses of Coke and set them on the bar. After paying for them, Eddie Kye picked up his half-empty beer mug.

"Let's go sit in a booth," he suggested.

Pete and Linc, carrying their glasses, followed him over to a rear booth. Kye took the seat facing the door, Linc slid in next to the wall facing him and Pete sat next to Linc.

The boys sampled their Cokes as Eddie Kye took a sip of his beer. Then the burly man said, "Scooter gave you some idea of what this is about, didn't he?"

"Yes, sir—I mean Eddie," Pete said. "When the track season starts, you want us to perform only as good as you tell us to. And we get paid for following orders."

"That's getting right to the point," Kye said with amused affability. "You got any idea why I'm willing to pay you for this?"

Linc said, "We figure you're planning to place some big bets on track and field events. But we also figure that's none of our business."

"That's the right attitude," Kye said approvingly. Then he deliberately let a tight, vaguely threatening smile replace his affable expression. "Part of the deal is that you keep your mouths shut. You never ask questions of either me or Scooter, and you don't tell even your best girls anything about the setup. If I find out you've got loose mouths, you not only get cut off the payroll, but you get lumps on your heads."

Linc cocked a quizzical eyebrow at him. Pete let his eyes narrow and said with faint belligerence, "We're no blabbers, mister, and you don't have to throw your weight around. You'd more likely get lumps on your own head, if you tried to put them on ours."

Eddie Kye's amused affability returned. "Cocky, ain't you, kid? It's all right, because I like cocky kids. I was just making a point. I guess you both understand it, so let's forget it and be friends, huh?"

"All right," Pete said, summoning an equally affable smile. "I was just making a point, too."

Linc said, "We know how to keep our mouths shut, Eddie. Don't worry about it. Let's talk about money."

"Sure," Kye said agreeably. "Scooter tells me you kids don't have no money at all to see you through the second semester."

Linc nodded, and Pete said, "Right."

"He figured tuition, fees, books and the cost of living in the dorm would run you about twelve-hundred each."

"About," Pete agreed.

"Usually payoffs are in lump sums for services rendered each time they're rendered," Kye said. "But Scooter says you kids won't even be in school next semester, unless you can be sure of some income. So I'm going to make an exception in your case and recommend you be put on a sort of retainer fee every month."

"Recommend?" Linc said. "To whom?"

"You're asking a question," Kye said with a frown. "I said no questions at all."

"Sorry," Linc told him. "How big a monthly retainer you plan to recommend? Or is even that kind of question out?"

"That one's okay. How would it grab you to draw fifty a month each for doing nothing until track season starts? You could bank it and have enough to keep you going the second semester, until the real money started coming in."

Pete said, "Fifty a month for the full school year only works out to 450 bucks each."

"It's only an advance," Eddie Kye explained. "Standard payoff for doing as you're told in a single event is two C's. In your case a hundred of the advance would be deducted each time until you're even. Then, if you got called on enough times, you'd start getting the full two hundred."

Pete and Linc looked at each other in pretended consultation. Linc nodded agreement. Pete turned back to Kye and said, "Okay. When's the fifty-a-month start?"

"Soon as I get an okay on it, which may be tonight. I'll try to have it start from the first of September."

"You've got a deal," Pete said, raising his Coke glass in a proffered toast to seal the contract.

Linc raised his Coke glass, too, and Eddie Kye

raised his beer mug. The three glasses touched, and all drank.

Kye set the beer mug down empty. Pete and Linc both drained their glasses, too. The burly man struggled his way out of the booth, having some difficulty getting out of the narrow seat because of his bulk.

"I guess that does it for now, kids," he said, glancing down at their empty glasses. "Either of you want refills?"

Both shook their heads and got out of the booth, also. Pete said, "Thanks, Eddie, but we still have some studying to do and we both have classes at 9 A.M."

"Better run then," Kye said, again turning on his affable smile and simultaneously clapping both on the shoulders. "We wouldn't want you guys to get grades too low to be eligible for track."

Eddie Kye was ordering another beer at the bar, when Pete and Linc went out.

As soon as they were outside, Linc said, "He mentioned he might get an okay on our deal tonight. Which means he must plan to contact the big man."

"Yeah," Pete said. "But maybe by phone."

Linc shrugged. "Maybe. But maybe personally, too. It's a fifty-fifty chance."

Pete rounded the Woody and slid in under the wheel. Linc climbed in the other side. Pete started the engine and pulled away.

"We're not going to take that fifty percent chance?" Linc inquired.

"We're not going to wait for him right in front of the door, where he couldn't avoid spotting us when he comes out."

He drove up Figueroa for one block, circled the block and parked on Ninth Street about a quarter block from Figueroa, at a point from where they could see the front door of Bertie's Bar and Grill. Pete checked his watch and saw it was just nine thirty.

At a quarter of ten, Eddie Kye emerged from the tavern. He climbed into the new Ford behind which the Woody had previously been parked. He drove south on Figueroa.

Pete let him get a half-block lead, then followed.

The Ford turned right at the next block, which was

Olympic Boulevard. It led them west on Olympic clear to the southern part of the enclave within Los Angeles known as Beverly Hills, which, although a separately-incorporated city, is completely surrounded by the larger city. They passed through all of Beverly Hills to emerge in the West Los Angeles District.

They were nearly to Santa Monica, when the Ford turned north on Barrington Avenue. They crossed Santa Monica Boulevard, and two blocks farther on the Ford turned right. As there was little traffic in this section, Pete let the interval between the two cars grow to a block. As they turned the corner, Linc peered out at the street sign.

"Rochester Avenue," he announced. "I figured that was where he was leading us."

"Yeah, so did I," Pete said.

A block ahead the Ford stopped and backed into a parking place. This was an area of apartment houses, and there weren't any parking places in the block where the Woody was. Pete double-parked and cut his lights.

The street was well enough lighted for them to be able to see Eddie Kye get out of his car, even though it was a block away, cross the street and enter an apartment building. Pete turned his lights back on and drove slowly past the building. Both he and Linc peered at the number on the building as they went by. It was easily read, because it was illuminated.

"Same address as is listed in Dinny Cord's package," Pete said with satisfaction. "I guess that removes any doubt about Dinny being the big man."

He drove to Santa Monica Boulevard, found a drugstore and phoned Captain Greer at his home, while Linc waited outside the booth.

When he had made his report, the captain said in a rare tone of approval, "Good work, Pete. When you learn when and where the first retainer fees are going to be paid to you, let me know, and we'll try to set things up so we can get photographic evidence of the payoff. Meantime, I think I'll put both Dinny Cord and Eddie Kye under twenty-four-hour surveillance."

"Good idea," Pete agreed. "We'll let you know as soon as we get word about our payoff."

CHAPTER 14

About the time Pete and Linc were meeting Eddie Kye at Bertie's Bar and Grill, Julie and Professor Barney Kuehn were just finishing dinner at a Chinese restaurant in New Chinatown.

Kuehn poured both of them more tea, while Julie opened her fortune cookie.

Pulling out the white slip, she read aloud, "New romance is coming into your life."

"Wrong tense," Kuehn corrected with a smile. "It should read: *has* come into your life."

She wrinkled her nose at him. "Read yours."

Kuehn broke open his cookie and drew out the fortune slip. "Beware of subordinates taking advantage of you," he read.

Then he looked up with a grin. "That's uncanny. They hit it right on the nose."

"You mean subordinates *are* taking advantage of you?" Julie asked with raised brows.

"Well, not exactly subordinates, but a couple of my history students. Not just of me, but of the whole college. Your old friends Cochrane and Hayes."

"Pete and Linc?" Julie said startled. "What do you mean?"

"They're fakes. They're in school on forged credentials." After a moment, he added, "Odd, too. They're both excellent students."

Julie marked time by taking a sip of her tea, while she unsuccessfully tried to think of some way to refute his charge. Finally she simply said, "How do you know?"

He sipped his own tea before saying, "Remember exactly a week ago tonight, when we were out for dinner,

I asked you how much you knew about Cochrane and Hayes?"

Julie nodded. "You asked me so many questions, I knew you suspected them of some kind of wrongdoing."

"Well, what made me suspicious was that after looking at the card on them that you have on file in the Athletic Department, I was impressed enough by their records to thumb through back issues of *Track and Field News* to see what was said about them. Are you familiar with the publication?"

"I've seen copies in the office," Julie said. "Frankly, I've never opened one."

"Well, it's just what it sounds like: a publication devoted to news about track and field from all over the country. Now Linc Hayes is supposed to run the hundred in 9.6 seconds, and is supposed to be able to throw the javelin 230 feet. Pete Cochrane is supposed to high jump six feet seven inches, and to long jump twenty-three and a half feet. None of those are records that would make headlines, but almost certainly they would be recorded in *Track and Field News*. I asked you all those questions last Tuesday night, because I hadn't been able to find mention of either one."

"Maybe that school in Missouri just didn't send in the news," Julie said hopefully.

The track coach shook his head. "Last Wednesday morning I sent an airmail inquiry to Central College. When I got home from school this afternoon, an airmail reply from the track coach was in my mailbox. Not only did Cochrane and Hayes never compete in track and field there, they were never even students."

Remembering Pete's suggestion, during last week's meeting in Mark Doyle's office, that Barney Kuehn be taken into their confidence if he managed to discover Pete and Linc weren't bona fide students, Julie wondered if she should reveal right now that the pair—and she—were cops. To conceal that she was furiously thinking, she took another sip of her tea.

After viewing the matter from all angles, she decided not to confess just yet, but instead to attempt to steer Kuehn to Mark Doyle, and let the athletic director break the news. With a touch of guilt she realized she wasn't making this decision as a policewoman, but simply as a woman. Quite candidly, she admitted to herself that she was afraid such an announcement might spoil the evening, and she rationalized that it wouldn't hurt anything, even from a police point of view, for Barney Kuehn not to discover she was a cop until morning.

"What are you going to do?" she finally asked.

"Report it to Dr. Vester in the morning."

"Don't you think you ought to talk it over with Mr. Doyle first?"

After considering, Kuehn said, "Perhaps. Actually this will be of more concern to Mark than to Dr. Vester. At least it's going to hit him harder. He was counting on those two to help me make a better track and field showing this year than we did last year. Do you expect Mark at the office first thing tomorrow morning?"

"At nine, yes."

"My first class tomorrow isn't until ten. I'll stop by to see Mark before I report to Dr. Vester."

"All right," Julie said, relieved. "I'll tell him to expect you."

It was past midnight when Julie got home from her date. She thought she ought to report that Barney Kuehn knew Pete and Linc were in school on forged credentials, but the boys had informed her that no one was on the dormitory switchboard after midnight. After stewing about it for a few minutes, she decided to phone Captain Greer's home, despite the late hour.

" 'Lo," the captain answered in a groggy voice that made it obvious that she had awakened him from a sound sleep.

"Sorry to call so late, Captain," Julie said contritely. "I got you out of bed, didn't I?"

"No," he said, sounding slightly more awake. "I'm still in it. I have a bedside phone." Then he came completely awake. "Hi, Julie. What's up?"

"Something happened tonight that I thought you ought to know." Quickly she explained her conversation with Barney Kuehn. "Maybe I should simply have told him Pete, Linc and I were all cops, and what we were investigating," she concluded. "I guess now he'll have to know, anyway. Instead I passed the buck to Mr. Doyle. Barney's coming to see him in the morning, before he reports his discovery to anyone else."

"Barney?" the captain said.

"Professor Kuehn," Julie amended primly.

"Oh. Well, you did all right, Julie. So long as he doesn't blab to anyone else on the campus before he gets to Doyle."

"He promised to come to the office first thing."

"All right, don't worry about it. I'm not sure all the coaches shouldn't have been taken into our confidence from the beginning. Dr. Vester's fear that one or more of them might be involved in this racket strikes me as extremely improbable."

"I think Mr. Doyle feels the same way," Julie said. "But he couldn't go against an order from the college president."

Captain Greer said, "Incidentally, Julie, Pete phoned me earlier tonight. He and Linc met with Eddie Kye this evening and set up a deal until track season starts, just so they'll be on tap when needed. Kye mentioned he had to get the agreement approved by a higher-up, so afterward the boys tailed him. He led them to the apartment house where Dinny Cord lives."

"Well now," Julie said in an interested voice. "I guess that makes it pretty definite that Cord is the mastermind of the racket, doesn't it?"

"I'd say so. But we still need proof. I'll try to catch the boys at the dorm before they leave for class in the morning, Julie, and tip them that their cover is blown insofar as Professor Kuehn is concerned. Or do they call him Barney, too?"

"Now, Captain," Julie said. "It doesn't become you to be coy."

Adam Greer chuckled. "All right, Julie. Good night."

"Good night, Captain," Julie said. "Again, sorry I awakened you."

The next morning, Julie found Professor Barney Kuehn waiting at the office, when she arrived at nine. Mark Doyle didn't come in until five minutes later, so she had no opportunity to alert the athletic director as to what was coming. After greeting both of them, Doyle took the track coach into his private office.

Only a couple of minutes passed before Doyle buzzed for Julie. She depressed the *Speak* switch on her intercom and said, "Yes, sir?" then depressed the *Receive* switch.

The athletic director's voice said, "Come in here, please, Julie."

She switched to *Speak* again, said, "Yes, sir," then turned both switches off.

When she entered the inner office, she closed the door behind her and remained next to it instead of advancing farther into the room. Mark Doyle was behind his desk, Barney Kuehn sat in a chair to the right of the desk, facing sideways. The athletic director had an amused smile on his face. The blond track coach looked faintly puzzled.

Julie nervously pushed a strand of hair back from her face and looked from one to the other.

Doyle said, "Professor Kuehn informs me that he has uncovered evidence that Peter Cochrane and Lincoln Hayes are in school under false pretenses."

"I know," Julie said. "He told me about it last night."

Kuehn regarded the athletic director with increasing puzzlement. "You seem to find it funny, Mark. Afraid I miss the joke."

Mark Doyle leaned back in his chair and clasped his hands across his stomach. "I guess the time has come to let you in on a little secret, Barney. I would have told you long ago, but I was instructed to take no one at all into my confidence except the police."

"The police? About what?"

"A week before school started, a co-ed named Eve Evans came to see me. Happen to know her?"

Barney Kuehn nodded. "She was in one of my classes last year. She goes with Scooter Miller."

"She used to go with him," Doyle corrected. "During the summer he threw her over for another girl. In revenge she came to me to report that last season Scooter had accepted bribes from a local gambler to lose events in at least three track meets."

"Scooter!" the track coach said in outraged astonishment.

"Scooter," Doyle confirmed. "She implied that he wasn't the only culprit, but that bribery throughout all our sports was widespread. However, Miller's was the only name she could give me. Or would give me, anyway. Naturally I took her story to Dr. Vester. His instructions were to attempt no personal investigation, to inform no one on campus and to turn the entire matter over to the police."

After absorbing this in silence for some seconds, Kuehn said slowly, "Cochrane and Hayes are cops, eh?"

"You guessed it," Doyle said.

The track coach gave Julie a puzzled look. "As old high-school friends, why didn't you know . . ." He broke off abruptly and let his eyes narrow.

Mark Doyle said with amusement, "You just guessed it again, Barney. She's a policewoman."

Barney Kuehn's face lost all expression. He merely continued to gaze at Julie silently.

In a self-conscious voice Julie said, "You know as much about the situation as I do, Mr. Doyle. You don't really need me, do you?"

"Not actually, I guess," Doyle said in an understanding tone.

Julie fled to the outer office, closing the door behind her. Then she came to an abrupt halt. An enormous red-haired youth, about six feet three inches in height and probably 250 pounds in weight, stood next to her desk.

From her intercom speaker Mark Doyle's voice came clearly, saying, "Of course, you'll be expected to keep this all in strict confidence, Barney. Dr. Vester . . ."

Julie cut off the rest by swiftly crossing to her desk and switching off the *Receive* switch.

CHAPTER 15

GAZING accusingly at the oversized red-haired boy, Julie said, "I distinctly remember turning that off. You've been deliberately eavesdropping."

The young man's face turned crimson. "Not me, lady," he said defensively. "I didn't hear anything. I just walked in this second. I didn't touch that contraption. I don't even know how to work it."

"What's your name?" she demanded.

"Larry Coons," he said meekly.

The name jolted her. The boy was Scooter Miller's roommate. If he had heard enough of the conversation in Mark Doyle's office to get the gist of it, the whole case was probably blown sky-high.

"Lancelot Coons, the fullback?" she said.

Larry Coons' face was already as red as it could get, but now it took on a stricken look. "I go by the name of Lawrence."

"Yes, I know. I saw how you signed your athletic record card." In a less imperious tone she inquired, "What do you want?"

"I just wanted to find out about student buses to Moorpark for Saturday's game."

"Aren't you going with the team?" she asked.

"Oh, sure. But my girl friend wants to go to the game. I'm finding out for her."

"Oh. The chartered buses leave from next to the field house at 11 A.M. Round-trip fare is two dollars."

"Thanks," Larry Coons said, and left hurriedly.

Another twenty minutes passed before Barney Kuehn emerged from the athletic director's office. When he paused before her desk, Julie gazed up at him timidly and self-consciously pushed a strand of hair back from her face.

"I think the term the students use is fuzz," he said. "I've been squiring around the fuzz."

"Sorry," she said, meekly lowering her eyes. "It wasn't my idea to fool you. I was under orders."

The blond man started to laugh. He laughed until tears formed in his eyes. Julie gazed up at him, at first uncomprehendingly, then with growing indignation.

When he finally stopped laughing long enough to wipe his eyes with a handkerchief, she said in an offended tone, "You find me funny, Professor Kuehn?"

"I find the situation hilarious." He paused to emit a final chortle. "The idea of dating a cop is pretty funny, you know. Particularly one who is secretly investigating your possible connection with a gang of criminals."

"I never suspected you of complicity," she indignantly denied. "That isn't why I went out with you."

"No?" he said, blue eyes twinkling. "Why was it?"

Raising her nose, she sniffed. "I was under the misapprehension you were nice. That was before I learned how funny you think girls are."

"Would you prefer me to get mad at you for fooling me?" he asked reasonably.

After studying his face, she let a smile gradually form on her own. "I guess being laughed at is better. And I suppose you deserve some revenge."

"Then we're still friends?" he inquired.

"If you like."

"I like," he said sincerely. "I'll pick you up for lunch as usual."

Then he glanced at his watch. "Holy smoke!" he said. "I have a ten-o'clock class, and it's three minutes to."

He headed for the door into the hall just as it opened, and Pete and Linc came in.

"Hi, fuzz," he said as he hurried past them and disappeared into the hallway.

When the automatic door-closer had allowed the door to swing completely shut, Pete said, "Did he say fuzz?"

"Yes," Julie said. "Did Captain Greer get hold of you this morning?"

"Uh-huh. I take it from the fuzz crack that Mark Doyle decided to tell the professor we were cops."

Julie nodded. "Barney isn't mad. In fact he's decided the idea of being investigated by the girl he's dating is funny. But our cover may be blown with more than just Barney."

Linc said, "How's that?"

"Mr. Doyle called me into his office while he was explaining things to Barney. When I came out, Larry Coons was standing next to my desk. I'm absolutely certain I had turned off my intercom, but it was on, and Mr. Doyle had left his key open. You could hear everything he was saying."

Pete and Linc both glanced at the closed door to Mark Doyle's office, then turned back to gaze at Julie in silence until she blushed.

"I didn't have the *Receive* switch open," she insisted. "He must have turned it on himself."

Pete made a dismissing gesture. "It's spilled milk, anyway. How much do you think he overheard?"

"He claimed that he had walked in just that second. But he also denied turning on the intercom, and I know it was off. If he could lie about one thing, he could lie about the other."

Linc said irritably, "What the devil was he doing here, anyway?"

"Oh, he just wanted some information. I think his reason for coming in was legitimate enough. It was just an unfortunate coincidence that he came in when he did."

"Well, there isn't anything we can do except wait and see what happens," Pete said. "If he overheard anything, we'll know soon enough, because he's bound to tell Scooter, and that will blow our cover completely."

Julie said hopefully, "Even if he heard enough to know an investigation is going on, he may not have heard the part about you boys and I being cops."

Linc asked, "Why? Was that only mentioned early in the conversation?"

After thinking, Julie gave her head a reluctant shake. "As a matter of fact, Mr. Doyle announced it toward the end. I guess if Coons heard anything, he heard that."

"Oh, fine," Pete said. "Larry may be looking for

Scooter right now to relay the news. Scooter will phone Eddie Kye, Eddie will contact Dinny Cord and everybody concerned will pull in their horns. Our case will go right down the drain."

Linc said, "Like you said, buddy-boy, all we can do is sweat it out. Don't get nervous before disaster happens. Meantime, think we ought to brief the captain on the possible disaster?"

"Why don't we wait until we learn whether or not it's going to be a disaster?" Julie suggested. "The captain can't do anything to divert it, and I'd just as soon miss the lecture, if no harm has been done."

"Now, Julie," Linc said with a grin. "You know Captain Greer only lectures us for our own good."

Pete said, "Julie's right, the captain couldn't do anything about the situation. So we may as well sit on it until we definitely find out our cover is blown."

They left it that way.

Pete and Linc didn't run into either Scooter Miller or Larry Coons all the rest of that day, despite keeping their eyes out for both. On a campus of three-thousand this wasn't surprising, since they had no classes with either boy, but they didn't encounter them in the dining hall or the dormitory either. Presumably, both had chosen to dine in the Student Union cafeteria or else off campus for both meals, beecause they didn't appear in the dining hall either for lunch or dinner.

If Scooter or Larry returned to the dormitory early in the evening, Pete and Linc had no way of knowing it, because they had arranged to meet Eve and Althea at the school library to study together immediately after dinner, and were there until it closed.

The library closed at 9 P.M. The boys walked the girls back to the girls' dormitory, stood talking for a few minutes outside the front door, then crossed the parking lot to the boys' dorm.

It was nine thirty when they let themselves into their room. Their door into the bathroom was open, but the one into Scooter Miller's and Larry Coons' room was closed. Pete switched on the bathroom light and opened the door. The other room was dark, but by the light from the bathroom he could see no one was in either bed.

He left both bathroom doors open when he returned to his and Linc's room.

"Still out," he announced.

At ten o'clock, they heard a key in the lock next door. Both boys were seated on their beds with pillows to their backs, finishing up the assigned reading they hadn't quite completed at the library. Both laid aside their books, but Linc remained where he was. Pete rose to go see which of their neighbors had come home.

Larry Coons had already come in and had closed the door behind him, when Pete reached the far bathroom door. Pausing in the doorway, Pete said, "Hi, Larry."

The big redhead glanced at him and immediately shifted his eyes away again. "Hi," he said shortly.

Coons slipped out of his jacket, hung it in his closet, sat on the edge of his bed and removed his shoes and socks. Pete watched him broodingly, but the fullback didn't look back at him.

Rising, Coons turned his back to pull down his bed and remove a pair of folded pajamas from beneath his pillow.

"Something eating you?" Pete asked.

Without turning around, Coons said, "I've the first football game of the season Saturday. I'm supposed to be in training, and it's my bedtime."

He unbuttoned his sport shirt, wadded it into a ball and tossed it into a corner, still with his back turned. He started to pull his T-shirt off over his head.

"Where's Scooter?" Pete inquired.

The fullback balled the T-shirt and fired it after the sport shirt. "Haven't seen him since lunch," he said shortly.

That dashed what little hope remained of retaining their cover. It was obvious from the fullback's manner that he had overheard everything said in Mark Doyle's office that morning. But Pete had been toying with the faint hope that if Coons hadn't seen his roommate, it might somehow be possible to talk him out of relaying what he had heard. Now, after Coons' intimation that he had lunched with Miller, that hope went glimmering.

As the big redhead started to take off his trousers,

still with his back turned, Pete said in a depressed voice, "Good night, Larry."

Coons didn't bother to reply. Pete drew the bathroom door closed behind him, crossed back to his own room and closed that door also.

"He didn't sound very friendly," Linc said.

"His back was to me during most of the conversation," Pete told him. "He knows we're cops."

"So what do we do now?"

"Phone Captain Greer in the morning and give him the bad news, I guess. No point in studying any more tonight, because we probably won't be students tomorrow. Want to play a game of cribbage?"

"You bring a board?" Linc asked.

"No."

"Neither did I. Make it gin rummy."

About ten minutes later, while they were playing gin rummy on Pete's bed, they heard the phone in the hall ring. Shortly afterward, there was a rap on the door. When Pete called, "It's open," a boy who lived up the hall near the wall phone stuck his head in.

"Phone for Linc Hayes or for Pete Cochrane if he's not available," he announced. "Some babe."

"Thanks," Linc said, rising. Then to Pete, "Probably Julie."

"Yeah," Pete said. He rose, too, and followed Linc up the hall to the phone.

When Linc answered, he was surprised to find it was Althea.

"Can you and Pete meet me and Eve in front of the girls' dorm right away?" she asked urgently.

"I guess," Linc said. "But what's up?"

"Scooter Miller is dead," Althea said. "He's been murdered. And Eve is nearly in hysterics."

CHAPTER 16

ALTHEA and Eve were waiting at the edge of the driveway that went past the girls' dorm, when Pete and Linc arrived. Eve threw herself against Pete's chest, buried her head on his shoulder and began to sob.

"Hey, cool it," he said soothingly, patting her shoulder. "Hold the tears until you tell us what it's all about."

"Scooter's dead," Eve said brokenly. "Somebody killed him."

"Who?"

She shook her head without raising her head from his shoulder. "I don't know. I didn't see."

"Well where, then?" Pete asked patiently.

"Near the chapel. We were sitting on one of the stone benches, when somebody came up behind us and stuck a knife in his back."

Since Pete had left the girl at the front door of the girls' dorm only a little over an hour ago, he was mystified as to why she had been half the length of the campus from there with another boy shortly afterward. But he tabled asking her to explain that, in favor of more urgent matters.

Taking her by both shoulders, he held her far enough away from him to look down into her tear-stained face. "Is he still there?" he asked.

She nodded, tears still rolling down her cheeks. "As soon as I saw the knife in his back, I ran. All the way back here."

"Are you sure he's dead?" Pete asked sharply.

Her eyes widened, and her tears stopped. "He didn't move," she whispered. "When I saw the knife, I just assumed . . ." She let it trail off.

Pete said, "First thing is to get to him. Dry your

eyes and straighten out, Eve. Maybe we can save him."

The suggestion that Scooter might not be dead after all had the effect of drying Eve's tears completely. Neither girl was carrying a handbag, but Eve had a handkerchief clutched in her hand. Pete waited until she had patted her eyes with it, then took her hand and started back across the parking lot at a fast walk. Linc and Althea hurried after them.

"Where you going?" Linc called.

"The Woody," Pete said succinctly.

The others instantly realized that it would be quicker to take the station wagon, even though there were no campus roads between here and the quadrangle. It was the equivalent of more than a city block to the quadrangle, but the main parking lot was just beyond it. It would be quicker to drive clear around the edge of the campus to the main lot than it would be to walk.

With Pete driving and Eve sitting next to him, and Linc and Althea in back, the Woody zoomed off the lot to the sidestreet beyond the men's dorm and headed south at high speed. Moments later it roared onto the main parking lot, deserted at this time of night, and across to the foot of the stone steps leading up to the administration building. Pete cut the motor and lights and grabbed a flashlight from the glove compartment. All four climbed from the station wagon and ran up the stone steps.

When they emerged onto the quadrangle from the arched passageway bisecting the administration building, Eve pointed in the general direction of the chapel forming the right side of the square, and said, "Over there."

The light from a globe burning in the roof of the arched passageway, plus a single globed bulb in the roof of the library porch faintly illuminated the central walk of the quadrangle leading from the arched passageway to the library, but to either side the shadow cast by trees created gradually thickening darkness. Near the liberal arts building to their left and near the chapel to their right, it was pitch black.

Pulling Eve along by the hand, Pete led the way in the indicated direction at a near trot, the beam of his flashlight probing ahead of them.

In front of a stone bench on the grass near the chapel Scooter Miller lay face down, arms and legs spread wide. The haft of what appeared to be a switchblade knife protruded from the left side of his back.

Althea emitted a little gasp and drew Eve away from the sight. Pete and Linc bent over the still figure.

Pete held his hand in front of Scooter's nose and mouth, but could feel no breath. He felt for the pulse behind the ear, but there was none.

Linc lowered his head to listen for a heartbeat. When he looked up again to give Pete an inquiring look, Pete shook his head.

"There isn't any heartbeat, either," Linc said.

Both boys rose to their feet. "You stay here," Pete suggested, handing Linc the flashlight. "I'll take the girls back to the dorm, get hold of a doctor and call the police."

"Okay," Linc agreed.

"All right, girls, let's get moving," Pete said crisply.

Taking Eve's hand, he started back across the quadrangle. Althea hurried after them.

"Is he . . . is he . . ." Eve faltered.

"Uh-huh," Pete said.

There was no more conversation until they reached the Woody. Both girls climbed in front, Eve in the middle.

As the station wagon roared toward the east exit from the lot, Pete said, "Want to tell me about it now, Eve? Start with how you happened to be there with Scooter."

"He was waiting for me in the dormitory sitting room, when you dropped me off tonight," Eve said. "At first I wasn't even going to talk to him, but he said it was urgent and almost pleaded, so I finally agreed to listen to what he had to say. Althea went on upstairs and left me with Scooter. He said he wanted to talk in private and suggested we take a walk. I really didn't want to, but he kept pleading, so I finally gave in. We walked down to the quadrangle and sat on that bench behind where he was lying."

During the short period she was speaking, the Woody had raced clear back to the boys' dormitory. As

Pete pulled onto the parking lot, he said, "What did he want?"

"He wanted for us to make up," Eve said. "He told me he had already broken up with the girl he's been going with—her name's Barbara Fenton—and that she'd created an awful scene earlier today, when he told her he was through with her. He also mentioned that he was in bad trouble, because the school knew about the bribes he had taken and was conducting an investigation, but how he found that out, I don't know. He only sort of threw that in to attempt to get my sympathy, I think. Mainly he was just interested in making up."

Pete pulled into his parking slot, cut the engine and lights, but didn't immediately get out of the car. "What did you tell him?" he asked.

"I said warmed-over love was like warmed-over steak: it never had the original favor. I told him there was no hope of us ever getting back together. While he was arguing for me to reconsider, a dim figure appeared behind us, and Scooter suddenly gave a pained grunt. I didn't see who it was. I was just vaguely conscious of someone coming up behind us, and by the time I turned around, whoever it was had disappeared again. Then Scooter pitched forward on his face, and I saw the knife in him."

"So you ran away?" Pete said.

"Yes," Eve admitted in a shamed voice. "I ran all the way back to the girls' dorm and up to our room. If any of the other girls had seen me, probably they would have thought I was crazy, but it just happened that the halls were deserted. I burst in, almost in hysterics, and finally Althea got me calmed down enough to tell her what had happened. Then she called you and Linc."

"Okay," Pete said. "Let's get inside to a telephone."

Luke Small didn't work the dormitory desk at night. A pudgy sophomore named George Yoder was behind the counter. He examined the two girls with Pete curiously.

Pete said, "Is there a doctor on call in case of emergencies in the dorm, George?"

"Sure. Dr. Custer's the school medic."

"Get him over here fast. Scooter Miller's been knifed."

"What?" the desk clerk said stupidly.

Pete lifted the hinged portion of the counter over the entry gate and stepped inside the enclosure.

"Just get him on the phone," he told Yoder. "I'll talk to him."

The pudgy youth consulted a list of emergency numbers posted next to the switchboard, rang one and handed his headset to Pete. After a couple of rings, a sleepy voice said in Pete's ear, "Dr. Custer."

Pete said, "This is Pete Cochrane, doctor, one of the residents of Howard Wayne Hall. Sorry to disturb you so late, but we have an emergency."

"Oh? Of what nature?"

"A boy has been stabbed."

All sleepiness disappeared from the doctor's voice. "I'll be right there."

"He isn't here, doctor. He's at the quadrangle, in front of the chapel. I'm pretty sure he's dead, but there may be some chance he isn't. How far away do you live?"

"Only about a block and half from the quadrangle. Have you called an ambulance?"

"No, sir."

"I'll have my wife call for one. Is anyone with the patient?"

"A student named Lincoln Hayes, doctor. He has a flashlight with him, so you won't need one."

"All right," Dr. Custer said. "Be there in ten minutes." He hung up.

"Now get me the police," Pete said to the pudgy desk clerk.

As Pete was reporting the matter to the police, dormitory manager Pop Henderson emerged from his apartment. When he saw the two girls, and Pete behind the counter with the clerk, he came over to see what was going on.

Pop Henderson, whose actual first name was unknown to Pete—or to most of the other dormitory residents—was a thin, timid-looking, chinless man of about sixty. Since the liberal rules adopted by the school administration for the men's dorm had left him virtually without authority over the residents, he was largely invisible. Usually, he was in evidence only at meal times in the dining hall, and otherwise stayed pretty close to the apartment he shared with his wife.

When Pete handed the headset back to George Yoder, Henderson said in a rather high-pitched voice, "Was that the police you were talking to, young man?"

"Yes, sir," Pete said. "Scooter Miller's been murdered."

Pop Henderson blinked. As Pete raised the hinged section to come out from behind the counter, the dormitory manager looked helplessly from Eve to Althea, then turned back to Pete.

"In the dormitory?" he squeaked.

Pete shook his head. "At the quadrangle. Dr. Custer is on his way there, and the police have been informed, so there's nothing more that has to be done."

"I see," Henderson said.

He rubbed his neck and continued to regard the girls somewhat owlishly until Pete introduced them. Then he diffidently inquired of Pete what the details of the tragedy were. When Pete had told what he knew, Henderson said he supposed the police would want to talk to him about breaking the news to the next of kin, so he wouldn't go to bed, as he had intended to.

"I'd suggest staying available for a while," Pete agreed dryly.

As he had instructed the police to go directly to the quadrangle, Pete drove the girls back to the main parking lot. A Buick sedan, which Pete assumed belonged to Dr. Custer, was parked at the foot of the stone steps leading up to the administration building. Pete left the girls in the Woody, while he went to check if it was the doctor who had arrived.

It was. Dr. Custer was a brisk, portly man in his forties wearing a suit coat over pajama tops. Linc was holding a light on the body while the doctor examined it.

Dr. Custer rose to his feet as Pete approached. Linc switched off the flashlight.

"I'm Pete Cochrane," Pete said. "It was I who phoned you."

Dr. Custer nodded. "I assumed that. We won't need

the ambulance when it arrives. He's dead. May as well leave the body just as it is, until the police get here."

"They're on their way," Pete said. "Where's the ambulance coming from?"

"I told my wife to phone the Central Receiving Hospital," Dr. Custer said.

Pete said, "Maybe when the police arrive, they can head it off by radio."

Linc said, "Did you get the story from Eve about what she was doing here with Scooter?"

"Uh-huh." Pete briefly outlined what Eve had told him. When he finished, he said, "I have the girls in the Woody. I'll go back and wait with them."

"Okay," Linc told him.

CHAPTER 17

As Pete descended the stone steps, a police radio car pulled onto the lot and drove over to park near the other two vehicles. A burly young patrolman and a lean, middle-aged sergeant got out.

Going over to them, Pete said in a low voice, "I'm Cochrane of the Mod Squad."

Both officers regarded him with interest. The older said, "This knifing report part of something you're working on?"

Pete said ruefully, "The victim was our main lead. I don't know if the knifing had anything to do with what we've been working on, though."

"Where is the victim?" the sergeant asked.

Pete nodded in the direction of the stone steps. "Up above. Everything's under control, though. Officer Hayes is up there, and also the school doctor. He just declared the victim dead. He had his wife phone Central Receiving for an ambulance before he got here. Maybe you could head it off."

"Sure," the sergeant said.

He called in on the car radio to cancel the order for the ambulance, and have a morgue wagon stand by for a call after Homicide officers had completed their investigation at the scene. Then he and his partner simply waited for the Homicide team to show up, deciding that since a police officer was already at the murder scene, it was unnecessary for them to stand by there.

Pete went over to lean in the window of the station wagon and tell the girls that Homicide investigators were on the way.

A few minutes later, an unmarked felony car arrived with the Homicide team. Pete was acquainted with both men. They were Sergeant Elbert (Bud) Dutton and Officer Hank Looper of the Homicide night trick. Dutton was a middle-aged, sleekly-groomed black man of average height and build. His partner was a long, lanky, towhead of about thirty, who looked like a backwoods rube dressed for church.

On the assumption that Pete was in some kind of undercover role, the detectives kept their greeting to him too low-toned for the girls seated in the station wagon to hear. In an equally low tone, Pete explained what had happened and that Linc and the school doctor were standing by at the murder scene.

"The girl who was with the victim when it happened is waiting over there," Pete finished, nodding toward the Woody. "The girl with her isn't a witness, and is just keeping her company. She's her roommate."

"We'll take a look at the scene first," Sergeant Dutton decided. "Could this have anything to do with whatever you guys are working on?"

"It's possible. We've been investigating a gambling ring that's been bribing Baldwin Hills athletes to hold down scores. The dead boy was one of the athletes involved. This morning, our cover was accidentally blown, and probably the victim informed his contact with the ring that we were cops. He may have been killed to be shut up."

He gave the two Homicide detectives a brief but detailed rundown on what they had so far uncovered about the gambling ring and its principals.

When he finished, Sergeant Dutton said, "Sounds

like a good motive. Did you say Captain Greer had stake-outs on Eddie Kye and Dinny Cord?"

"He said he was going to arrange it."

"Then checking them out ought to be simple. The stakeouts should be able either to alibi them or place them at the scene of the crime. How about this runner, Johnny Merlin?"

"The captain didn't mention putting him under surveillance."

The black detective gave his head a gloomy shake. "That's too bad. He's been doing hatchet work for Dinny Cord on and off for years, and if Cord ordered the hit, he was probably the hitter." He turned to the uniformed sergeant. "When the lab boys arrive, send them on up, Sam."

"Sure," the sergeant said.

Pete accompanied the two Homicide officers up the stone steps, through the arched passageway and across the quadrangle to where Linc and Dr. Custer stood near the body. The detectives introduced themselves with no sign of recognition for Linc, then Bud Dutton asked the doctor for his report.

"I imagine he died instantly," the doctor said. "The blade entered the heart from the rear. It seems to have passed between two ribs, so the thrust didn't necessarily require much force. I mention that, in case you planned to ask my opinion as to whether a man or woman stabbed him. I couldn't guess."

"Could you guess if the assailant was right or left-handed?" Dutton asked.

Dr. Custer shook his head. "Depends on just where he was standing when he struck. You could probably get a more valid opinion from the girl who was with him."

"Okay, Doctor," the black sergeant said. "Thanks for your trouble. We can get a copy of the death certificate from the coroner's office after you file it, so we won't need you anymore tonight, if you want to go home."

"Then I'll do that," Dr. Custer said, stooping to pick up his medical bag from where it lay on the grass. "Good night, gentlemen."

When the doctor had departed, the Homicide officers examined the body by flashlight without touching it.

"The doctor didn't move it," Linc offered. "It's just as it was."

Bud Dutton grunted. Both he and his partner had brought flashlights, and now they began a methodical study of the area around the bench in gradually widening circles. They paid particular attention to the area between the bench and the chapel, but seemed to find nothing of interest.

"The assailant could have ducked behind that tree there," Sergeant Dutton said, shining his light on the thick bole of a tree only a few yards behind the bench. "Then he could have kept the tree between himself and the bench until he reached the north corner of the chapel and ducked around it."

Hank Looper said, "Yeah, probably what happened."

A civilian photographer and a fingerprint technician arrived then. Dutton told the photographer what pictures he wanted and asked the technician to dust the knife handle for fingerprints. The black man left his partner to supervise these operations, while he went back down to the parking lot to question Eve. Pete and Linc went along with him.

Eve told substantially the same story she had told Pete. The only addition was that when Sergeant Dutton asked if she suspected anyone in particular, she hazarded that it might have been Barbara Fenton.

"The only evidence I know of against her is that Scooter said she made a scene, when he told her they were through," Eve admitted frankly. "And women sometimes do kill men who reject them. I don't mean this as an accusation so much as merely a suggestion of one place to look."

"We'll check her out," the black Homicide detective assured her.

Hank Looper, the fingerprint man and the photographer all came down the steps together. Looper was carrying the knife. He got a manila envelope from the car he and Dutton had come in, tagged the knife as evidence and put it in the envelope. He locked the envelope in the car trunk.

The fingerprint man reported that there had been only smudges on the knife handle, none clear enough to bring out. The photographer reported that he had taken all the pictures Dutton had told him to.

Dutton told both of them they could go, then said to the middle-aged sergeant in uniform, "May as well call for the morgue wagon now, Sam. You and your partner can stand by until it comes for the body, then you can take off."

"Okay, Bud," the sergeant said. "Will do."

Sergeant Dutton told Pete and Linc that he wanted to talk to the dead boy's roommate, and also to the dormitory manager, but that he wouldn't need Eve anymore that night, and the boys could take her and Althea to the girls' dorm. They drove the girls back to the dorm, then Pete parked the Woody in its usual slot on the parking lot, and he and Linc met the two Homicide officers in front of the men's dorm.

They noted that Hank Looper had the manila envelope containing the knife with him.

Although by now it was a few minutes past midnight, young George Yoder was still on duty at the desk. Apparently this was because the hallway and lobby were so crowded with students that he had decided to stay open overtime. News of the murder had spread through the dormitory, bringing a large number of residents out front in search of details. They stood about in groups, discussing the matter.

Attention focused on Pete, Linc and the two Homicide detectives when they came in. Pop Henderson made his way through the crowd of students and asked Dutton and Looper if they were police officers.

The pair told him they were and showed their I.D.s.

The dormitory manager's main concern seemed to be about contacting and breaking the news of their son's death to Scooter Miller's parents in Bakersfield. He was obviously relieved when Dutton told him he would take care of it, if Henderson would give him the information as to how to get in touch with them. Henderson already had the data written on a piece of paper. He gave it to the detective.

The towering Art Feister was in the crowd, although his Mexican-American roommate wasn't in evidence.

Pushing his way to the front, he said to Pete and Linc, "Did you tell the police about the threat Dewey Stockton made against Scooter?"

"What was that?" Bud Dutton asked alertly, looking from Pete to Linc.

"He's talking about the president of the Afro-American Student Union," Linc said. "The AASU planned to take over the school administration building to force certain demands the other day, but it was full of cops when they got there. Dewey blamed Scooter Miller for tipping them off, and he said he'd get even. But he was just sounding off. It wasn't the sort of thing you'd kill somebody for."

"How do you know what a hot-headed radical like Dewey Stockton would consider justifiable murder?" the basketball star demanded. "He's out somewhere tonight, and his roommate doesn't know where he is."

"You checked on him when you heard about the murder, huh?" Pete said.

"Sure, I checked on him," Feister said belligerently. "Why shouldn't I?"

In a dry tone Linc said to Bud Dutton, "There's some philosophical disagreement between Dewey and Art here. Art sort of represents the Establishment."

"I gathered that," the black Homicide officer said. "We'll still want to check this Dewey Stockton out, though. Is his roommate in the crowd?"

Pete and Linc both glanced around. "Don't see him," Pete said. "We'll show you his room." Then he looked around again and asked, "Did anyone get Larry Coons up?"

Since no one answered, presumably the fullback was still sleeping.

"Coons is the victim's roommate," Pete informed Dutton. "You said you wanted to talk to him."

"Let's take care of another detail first," Hank Looper suggested. Removing the still-open-bladed and blood-stained knife from the manila envelope, the lanky detective held it aloft so that everyone in the crowd could see it. Raising his voice, he called, "Anyone recognize this weapon?"

There was a considerable amount of murmuring, but no one admitted ever having seen the knife before.

After a few moments, Looper replaced it in the envelope.

"Okay, let's go wake up this Coons boy," Dutton said.

CHAPTER 18

PETE pointed out the room occupied by Dewey Stockton and Arnie Trotter as they went past it, but Sergeant Dutton preferred to table the president of the AASU until later.

When they all entered room 244, Pete led the way through the bathroom into the room connecting with his and Linc's. When he switched on the overhead light, Larry Coons sat up in bed and blinked around stupidly at his four visitors.

"What's the idea?" he inquired in a surly voice.

"This is Sergeant Dutton and Officer Looper of the LAPD Homicide Division, Larry," Pete announced. "They want to ask you a few questions."

"Homicide Division?" the big redhead said, his eyes widening and his expression becoming alert. "Has there been a murder?"

"Uh-huh. Your roommate."

"Scooter!" Coons said with shocked disbelief.

When Pete merely nodded, Coons rolled out of bed, shoved his feet into a pair of slippers and lifted a maroon robe from the foot of his bed. Slipping on the robe, he sat on the edge of his bed and looked from Sergeant Dutton to his tow-headed partner. Aside from his face turning somewhat pale, he seemed to have absorbed the shock of the announcement pretty well.

"It happened a couple of hours ago," Dutton said. "Over on the school quandrangle. Your roommate was sitting on one of those stone benches with a girl, when somebody sneaked up behind them and shoved a knife in his back."

"Who?"

Dutton shook his head. "We don't as yet know. It was pitch dark, and the girl didn't see the killer."

"Barbara wasn't hurt?" Larry asked.

Pete said, "He wasn't with Barbara. He was with Eve Evans."

The redhead looked astonished. "Eve? How come?"

Pete said, "According to her, he was begging her to take him back."

Larry Coons thoughtfully scratched the nape of his neck. "He must really have been mad at Barb. They been fighting for the past couple of days, you know. I don't know what she's been bugging him about, but it had him sore enough so that he was talking about telling her to get lost. I never figured he'd go back to Eve, though, even if he and Barb did break up."

Dutton said, "Show him the weapon, Hank."

Looper produced the knife from its manila envelope and showed it to Coons. The fullback denied ever seeing it before. Looper put it away again.

"When did you last see your roommate?" Dutton asked.

"At lunch today. We ate together in the Student Union cafeteria."

Pete said, "During lunch I suppose you told him about the conversation you overheard in the athletic director's office this morning."

"What conversation?" Coons asked evasively.

Pete said, "Look, Larry, if Scooter told his gambler friends that the police knew about Baldwin Hills athletes being bribed, one of them may have slipped that knife in him to shut him up. So what you told him may have killed him."

The fullback looked upset by the suggestion, but he made no comment.

Linc said, "Come on, Lancelot, how about a little cooperation?"

Larry Coons gradually turned beet red. "Who told you about that?" he demanded to know.

"We looked at your athletic record card," Linc told him. "Does your redheaded girl friend know your name is Lancelot?"

Coons gazed at him in consternation. "You wouldn't tell her," he whispered.

"We won't tell anybody if you cooperate," Linc said cheerfully. "If you don't, we'll spread it all over the campus. You want to help us out?"

"What do you want to know?" Coons inquired in a husky voice.

"We'll start with this morning. How much did you overhear?"

The redhead's face began to regain its normal color. "Enough to know what the meeting was about," he said in a reluctant tone. "It was pure accident. I really wasn't trying to listen in. I was standing there waiting for somebody to show up, and I happened to spot the intercom. Just because I didn't have anything to do, I sort of idly pushed one of the switches. It shook me up when I heard Mr. Doyle's voice coming out of the speaker. But when I heard him say that you and Pete and the new girl he has working for him were all cops, I left it on and listened. Then the girl came out and caught me."

"Did you catch what it was that brought us to the campus?" Pete asked.

"Sure. Guys taking bribes to throw games."

"I mean what originally started the investigation."

Coons shook his head. "Guess I missed that. What did?"

Pete saw no point in divulging that Eve Evans had blown the whistle on Coons' roommate. Instead of answering the question, he asked one of his own. "What was Scooter's reaction, when you told him what you had overheard?"

"First, he was sore at you guys. Then he began to get scared at how Eddie Kye would take having a pair of cops steered to him. He said he'd better get to Eddie fast and advise him to drop out of sight for a while."

Bud Dutton said, "Do you know if he contacted Kye?"

"He said he was going to right after lunch."

"Do you know Eddie Kye personally?" Hank Looper asked.

Coons shook his head. "I just know the name from

Scooter mentioning it. I wasn't involved in this bribery deal, you know."

"Oh, come on, Larry," Pete said. "Don't try to snow us."

"I wasn't," the fullback insisted. "I'm not saying I didn't know anything about it, because Scooter tried to talk me into getting involved. Anybody else I would have reported, but how can you fink on your own roommate and best buddy for something you know will get him expelled?"

"So you just let it go on?" Linc said unbelievingly. "Even though you knew some of your teammates were deliberately throwing points?"

"Only suspected," Coons said quickly. "After turning down Scooter's proposition, by mutual agreement we never mentioned the matter again. I didn't want to know which other athletes were involved. I have to admit I suspected there were quite a few. I think Scooter got some kind of bonus for each one he lined up who was willing to cooperate. But I never talked to him about it."

Bud Dutton said, "I'm not particularly concerned about whether you were on the take or not, Coons. Let's get back to the murder. Were you here in your room all evening?"

The fullback shook his head. "I came in about ten." He nodded toward Pete and Linc. "These guys saw me come in."

"That's right," Pete confirmed. "It was about ten."

"About fifteen minutes after your roommate was killed," the black Homicide officer said. "Where were you coming from?"

Coons scowled at him. "You don't suspect me of killing Scooter, do you?"

"Just answer the question, please."

Coons shrugged, but the scowl remained on his face. "I'd been over to the Petöfi Club with my girlfriend."

"That's a student hangout only a couple of blocks from here," Pete put in.

Dutton nodded. "What's your girl's name?"

"Patty Lathrop."

The black man glanced at his rubelike partner, who took out a small notebook and wrote the name down.

Pete said, "She rooms in the girls' dorm with the Barbara Fenton whom Eve Evans mentioned."

Bud Dutton nodded again. "We'll check both of them out." To Coons he said, "Had you just dropped Miss Lathrop off before you came home?"

"About five minutes before. It takes that long to walk across the parking lot."

"I guess that does it," Dutton said. He glanced at his partner again. "You have anything more, Hank?"

When Looper shook his head, Dutton said, "Then let's go see if the Stockton kid is in yet."

Linc said, "One last thing. Larry, did you mention to anyone but Scooter that Pete and I were cops?"

Coons gave his head a negative shake. "Not even Patty."

"Good," Linc told him. "That's part of the deal about your name. You keep quiet about that, and nobody will find out Larry is a nickname for Lancelot."

"I'm not going to tell anybody," Coons said aggrievedly.

When Pete, Linc and the two Homicide officers emerged into the hallway, the satanic-looking Dewey Stockton was just coming up the stairs. They met him in front of the door to his room.

Dewey had already learned of the murder from the students still gathered downstairs, so he showed no surprise when Linc introduced Dutton and Looper as Homicide officers. To Dutton's question as to where he had been all evening, he said he had attended a movie alone.

"Which one?" Dutton asked.

"Why?" Dewey inquired. "Am I a suspect?"

"Well, we have information that you made a threat against the victim."

"Me?" the goateed black youth said in what sounded like honest surprise. "Who told you that?"

Linc said, "He's talking about last Thursday morning, Dewey, when you sounded off about getting even with Scooter, because Rogers Memorial Hall was full of cops."

Dewey gave Linc a reproachful look. Linc said, "Don't look at me or Pete. Art Feister finked on you."

"Oh," Dewey said. "I might have suspected that. He's as square as Scooter was. You know I was only talking off the top of my head, Linc. I wouldn't kill anybody for a thing like that."

"Just what I told the officers here, Dewey," Linc told him with a shrug. "But they get paid to ask questions."

Dewey searched his jacket pockets and produced the stub of a movie ticket. He handed it to Bud Dutton.

Examining it, the black man said, "Granada Theater. That's over on 39th Street, isn't it?"

"Uh-huh," Dewey said.

"What was playing?"

"A rerun of *Gone With the Wind*."

Dutton regarded him dubiously. "Ever see it before?"

"This was my third time. So it wouldn't prove anything for you to ask me what it was about."

"No," the sergeant agreed. He turned to Hank Looper. "Show him the murder weapon, Hank."

Looper withdrew the knife from its manila envelope. Dewey made a face when he saw it.

"Ever see this before?" Looper asked.

The bearded black youth shook his head. "Never," he said positively.

Looper returned the knife to the envelope.

Bud Dutton said, "That's all for now, Stockton. Just stay available, huh?"

"Sure," Dewey said. "I'm not planning to go anywhere."

He keyed open his door, went inside and pulled it closed behind him.

"I guess you guys can go to bed, too," Dutton told Pete and Linc.

"Aren't you going to question Barbara Fenton and Patty Lathrop tonight?" Pete asked.

"Sure, we're going to wake them up. But we don't need you along."

Linc said, "How would Bud and Hank explain dragging a couple of male students along to question residents of the girls' dorm in the middle of the night, genius? Everybody would know we were cops, too."

"Yeah, I guess," Pete said ruefully. "My curiosity

was pushing me, but this really isn't our baby. Okay, guys, we'll leave the rest of it in your capable hands."

Bud Dutton grinned at him. "We'll try to manage. You and Linc have been big helps, though. Maybe we'll ask Captain Greer to let you continue to give us a lift."

"Oh, joy," Linc said. "We'll get to stay in school after all."

CHAPTER 19

EARLY Thursday morning, Pete phoned Captain Greer to report developments. The captain had just arrived at his office and had not previously heard of Scooter Miller's murder.

When Pete finished his report, Captain Greer said, "You figure your cover is still intact as far as the students are concerned, eh?"

"Except for Larry Coons. And we're pretty sure he won't blow it."

"I don't see what good that will do, if Miller told Eddie Kye you were cops," Greer complained. "Julie really loused up this case with her blasted intercom."

"It wasn't her fault, Captain. If you want to fix blame, pin it on Mark Doyle for leaving his *Speak* switch open."

"Well, in any event it's likely that Eddie Kye and Dinny Cord will pull in their horns so far that we'll never be able to link them to the briberies now. About all you can hope to salvage from your investigation is to find out what athletes have been accepting bribes by working on the athletes themselves."

Pete said dubiously, "You mean by trying to work our way into their confidence and getting them to confess?"

"I don't care what methods you use," the captain said peevishly. "All I'm concerned about is results."

"Yes, sir," Pete said. "Homicide Division may want our help on this murder case, too. Bud Dutton mentioned last night that he might contact you about it."

"Oh?" Captain Greer said. "In that case, maybe you'd just better mark time until we see what develops in that connection. Why don't you check back with me about noon?"

"Yes, sir," Pete said.

When he emerged from the booth, Linc, who had been waiting outside, gave him a look of inquiry.

"We're to mark time and check back with him at noon," Pete said.

Linc shrugged. "Then we may as well make our classes."

When Pete phoned Captain Greer again at noon, the captain said, "Martinez and Bidder of the Homicide day trick have the follow-up on the Miller murder, and they've requested an assist from the Mod Squad. I've set up a conference in my office for 3 P.M. Contact Julie and have her arrange with Mark Doyle to get away from the office for it."

"Yes, sir," Pete said. "Any developments on the murder case?"

"Several, but you'll hear all about it at three."

"Yes, sir," Pete repeated.

When Pete stepped out of the booth, Linc said, "That was short."

"But not sweet. The captain was in one of his crisp moods. Martinez and Bidder have the follow-up on the Miller kill, they've requested our help and we're all to meet in the captain's office at three."

"Julie, too?"

"Uh-huh, but she's probably at lunch now. We'll drop by and see her after lunch."

Julie had no trouble arranging to get away from the office. She had already heard of the murder when the boys contacted her, because news of it had spread all over the campus, but of course she didn't know the inside details of the investigation. En route downtown, Pete and Linc briefed her on everything that had occurred the previous night.

Although they arrived at Captain Greer's office five

minutes early, they found Sergeant Miguel (Mike) Martinez and Officer Lee Bidder already there. The Mexican-American sergeant was a tall, exceedingly handsome man of impeccable grooming. His partner, Lee Bidder, was slow-moving and gangling, and deliberately cultivated a vacant expression, because he had found it invaluable when questioning suspects. It tended to make them overconfident of their ability to fool him. Both men were about thirty years old.

After general greetings had been exchanged and the new arrivals had found seats, Captain Greer said, "Before Mike and Lee start their briefing, I want to bring you up to date on the activities of Eddie Kye and Dinny Cord. Several days ago I asked Intelligence Division to put both under surveillance, you know."

Pete said, "Yeah, I remember you saying you intended to."

"About one thirty yesterday afternoon, a young man visited Eddie Kye's apartment. From the stakeout's description of him, it was Scooter Miller. The young man stayed only about fifteen minutes. Shortly after he left, Kye emerged from his apartment, climbed into his car and drove off. He pulled some fancy evasive maneuvers and managed to shake his tail. What does that indicate to you?"

Julie looked puzzled. Pete was still thinking it over, when Linc said, "It indicates that Scooter had told him Pete and I were cops. It's doubtful that Eddie actually spotted his stakeout, because those Intelligence guys are too good. The tail would have been invisible. Ergo, he just assumed a tail was probably on him, because he knew the cops were investigating him."

Captain Greer nodded. "Exactly. I think we can accept as a certainty that Kye is aware you and Pete are cops. Also that he relayed the information to Dinny Cord, because that's where he headed after shaking his tail. He was picked up again by the stakeout at Cord's apartment when he showed there."

Pete shrugged. "We figured our cover was blown with both of them anyway, Captain."

"I haven't finished," Captain Greer said. "When the stakeout on Dinny reported in by radio that Eddie Kye had showed there, Eddie's tail rushed over to pick him up. But when Eddie left there, he again went through some fancy maneuvers and shook the tail a second time. Shortly afterward, Dinny Cord left his apartment and drove off, too. And guess what?"

Julie said, "He lost his tail, too."

"Right. Neither one has been located since. Obviously, they've both gone into hiding to avoid questioning about the briberies."

"Or about the murder," Linc suggested.

Mike Martinez said, "Yeah, they could be involved in that. If they hadn't shaken their tails, they would both have perfect alibis for the time of the murder—providing neither pulled it. Now they're both prime suspects."

Captain Greer said, "Go ahead and explain what you have so far on the murder investigation, Mike."

The handsome Mexican-American nodded. "First I'll bring you up to date on what Dutton and Looper accomplished, before they turned the case over to us. After they left the men's dorm last night, they had the house mother at the girls' dorm get Barbara Fenton and Patty Lathrop out of bed. The Lathrop girl confirmed Larry Coons' story that he was with her all evening and left her at the girls' dorm about five minutes to ten. So he's off the hook as a suspect."

"How'd Barbara react to the news that her boyfriend was dead?" Pete inquired.

"She threw a fit of hysterics, which Bud Dutton suspects was faked. Hank Looper disagrees with him, but I have more respect for Dutton's ability to evaluate suspects than I have for Looper's."

"Why would she pretend hysterics?" Julie asked puzzledly.

"She wouldn't have any reason to unless she already knew Miller was dead."

Julie's eyes widened. "You mean she might have actually done what the Evans girl suggested?"

"Here is the evidence against her," Martinez said, ticking each point off on his fingers as he listed it. "Item one, she admitted having a running fight with Miller that lasted several days, and ended with him telling her he was through with her. It was over his accepting bribes, she says. Miller seems to have had a bad habit of confessing all to his girl friends, because he told this one all his business, too."

"It's a wonder he lived as long as he did," Pete commented, which Julie apparently took as a slur on womanhood, because she made a face at him.

Martinez said, "Barbara claims she was insisting that Scooter break off his relationship with Eddie Kye, but that he wouldn't. He finally got tired of her bugging him and kissed her off. End of item one. Item two, she wasn't in her room when her roommate entered it just before ten last night, but came in a few minutes later. And her roommate describes her as extremely distraught. Item three, she admits seeing Scooter Miller and Eve Evans leave the girls' dorm together and walk off into the darkness. As a matter of fact, she claims that's what made her distraught."

"Well, couldn't that be?" Julie asked.

"It could be," the sergeant admitted. "Except her explanation of where she was during the approximate half hour from then until she returned to the dorm isn't very plausible. She says she was so upset at the sight of her boyfriend and his former steady walking off hand-in-hand that she wandered off blindly in the opposite direction. She says she walked clear up to the field house and sat on a bench there in the dark, crying."

"A plausible enough feminine reaction," Julie said.

Martinez frowned at her. "Seems more plausible to me that a jealous woman would follow her rival and her boyfriend to see where they were going."

"That's because you think like a man and men are sneakier than women," Julie told him.

Captain Greer, Pete and Linc all gave her quizzical smiles. Lee Bidder said, "Psychological considerations aside, Julie, you have to admit she had the best opportunity of any suspect. Who else knew Scooter would be seated on that bench?"

Linc said, "Aw, come on, Lee. Anybody could have been tailing him."

"Wouldn't the Fenton girl have spotted a tail?" Bidder argued. "She claims she watched them walk off, until they were out of sight."

Linc shrugged. "That's pure conjecture. Maybe it was a smart tail."

Mike Martinez said, "At any rate, she *could* have followed them. And if she overheard Scooter pleading with Eve Evans to take him back, jealousy might have induced her to slip that knife into him."

"There's one huge hole in your case," Julie said. "Whoever heard of a nice, middle-class college girl carrying around a switchblade knife?"

"We thought of that," Martinez admitted. He glanced at Linc. "I don't often spout generalities about racial traits, Linc, but I think the one I'm about to spout has some validity. Don't you agree that traditionally males of your race have been more likely to routinely carry cutting weapons than white co-eds have?"

"I wouldn't argue against that," Linc said with a grin. "I won't even class it as a bigoted remark. You're talking about Dewey Stockton, I assume."

"Uh-huh. He's our next most likely suspect. Lee and I looked up the Granada Theater's manager this morning. According to him the ticket bearing the number on Dewey Stockton's stub had to be sold around 8 P.M. The show ran four hours, from eight until midnight. Stockton may have sat through it, or he may have merely bought the ticket to create an alibi. He could have walked in the front door and right out a side exit."

Captain Greer said, "So, altogether you have four good suspects. Eddie Kye, Dinny Cord, Barbara Fenton and Dewey Stockton. Is that it?"

"Uh-huh," the Mexican-American said.

Pete said, "Seems to me you left one out."

"Who?" Martinez asked.

"Johnny Merlin, the deliveryman for the Cord Laundry and Cleaning Company, who doubles as a runner for Dinny Cord. Bud Dutton suggested that if Dinny ordered the hit, Merlin quite likely was the one who did the hitting."

Lee Bidder said, "He suggested it to us, too, Pete. So we checked Johnny out. At the time of the murder, he was at a wedding reception with two hundred other people."

Pete said, "Oh."

"We didn't talk to all two hundred, of course," Bidder said. "We quit after four verified that he was there."

Captain Greer said, "Any chance of tracing that knife?"

Mike Martinez shrugged. "We got off a letter to the manufacturer asking for a list of local outlets, but it's a mass-produced item. It's doubtful that we'll be able to trace it."

"How are we going to fit into the investigation?" Pete asked. "What do you want us to do?"

Martinez said, "I thought you might go to work on the Fenton girl, while Linc works on Dewey Stockton. Maybe one or the other will confess."

Pete made a face. "You expect me to romance the girl and then sell her out?"

"How about me?" Linc inquired. "The man's asking me to fink on a soul brother."

In a testy voice, Captain Greer said, "That kind of moral scruples is incompatible with your undercover roles. You think murderers deserve Marquis of Queensbury treatment?"

"We're just exercising the traditional American privilege of griping, Captain," Pete told him. "We'll get the job done."

"What am I supposed to do?" Julie asked.

"Stay where you are as Mark Doyle's secretary," Captain Greer instructed her. "This murder investigation is merely an additional assignment, it doesn't supercede your original mission. We're still after the names of the Baldwin Hills athletes who have accepted bribes."

CHAPTER 20

BARBARA FENTON was in Pete's physics class, but on Friday she was absent. Early in the afternoon, somewhat hating himself, Pete dropped by the girls' dormitory and asked for her.

The glamorous platinum blonde came downstairs wearing blue Levi's, and a man's shirt slightly too large for her. Her feet were bare, with clear polish on the nails. She looked a trifle surprised when she saw who her visitor was.

Pete said, "Hi, Barb. I noticed you were absent from physics today and thought you would like the assignment."

He handed her a slip of paper on which he had written the assignment.

"Oh, thanks," the girl said. "I haven't been attending class the last couple of days, since. . . ."

When she let it trail off, Pete said, "Since Scooter's death, you mean. We were all sorry about that."

Barbara's eyes momentarily moistened, but then she sternly held back tears. Folding the slip of paper Pete had given her, she stuck it in the breast pocket of her shirt and said, "Thanks again."

"Maybe it would do you good to get out," he suggested. "Like to run over to the Petöfi Club for a while?"

She shook her head. "Thanks, but I couldn't stand to be among all those chattering kids."

"Well, how about just a quiet ride? Or a walk?"

She examined him speculatively, then nodded agreement. "Maybe a walk would do me good. I'm tired of staring at walls. Can I go like this?"

Pete smiled down at her bare feet. "Sure. We'll avoid gravel roads."

Outside Pete let Barbara pick the direction, and she turned north toward the Student Union. They walked along in silence for a few moments.

As they crossed the driveway circling past the girls' dorm and stepped onto the grass beyond it, Pete said, "You're going to have to get over it and start attending classes again soon, Barbara. I know it's rough, but you'll flunk out of school."

"I plan to start back to classes Monday," she said.

"You're blaming yourself because you'd been fighting with Scooter, aren't you?" he said. "It's given you a guilt complex."

She looked at him strangely. "I never mentioned to anyone but Patty Lathrop that Scooter and I had a fight—except the two detectives who investigated his death. How do you know about it?"

Pete said easily, "Scooter told Larry Coons about it. Larry told me."

"Oh." They walked on several yards before she asked, "Do you know what the fight was about?"

"Sure. You wanted Scooter to quit taking bribes to throw track events."

"Larry certainly confides in you," she said with a frown.

"Well, he was aware I knew all about the bribes, anyway. Scooter tried to line me and Linc up with the same guy who was paying him off."

Barbara looked surprised. "With Eddie Kye?"

"I think that was the name he mentioned. Linc and I never went through with the deal, incidentally, so you won't have to work on me to reform like you did on Scooter."

She glanced at him sideways. "I don't know that I'll ever again give any boy moral advice. Maybe I *was* being a shrew."

Not quite sure what this allusion meant, Pete made no comment. They neared the Student Union but went on past it, when Barbara gave no indication of desiring to stop there.

Presently the girl said, "From the free way Larry talked about the bribes to you, it sounds as though he was accepting them, too. He told Patty he wasn't."

"He told me that, too," Pete said. "Whether he was or not, I don't know. But he definitely knew all about Scooter's involvement."

For a time they walked in silence. Finally, she said in a depressed tone. "If only we hadn't parted that last time on such bad terms. I would like something better to remember than those awful things he said to me."

"When was that?"

"That morning, between classs, when he met on the quad. I made the mistake of mentioning the bribes again, and he blew right up. He said he was tired of being bugged, and called me a shrew. He said if I wanted a man I could henpeck, to get another, because he'd had it right to the eyebrows. Then he walked off before I could even answer. I never saw him again except from a distance that night."

"You mean when he was with Eve?" Pete asked.

"Yes. I saw them from my room window. It upset me so much, them walking off hand-in-hand like that, I ran downstairs and outside and gazed after them until they disappeared from sight. That's another last memory that isn't very pleasant."

Pete said, "I was on friendly terms with Scooter, so I don't mean to slight his memory, but it seems to me he treated you pretty badly. Why don't you just try to forget him?"

"I was in love with him," she said simply.

There was another period of silence, this one stretching until they reached and started past the athletic administration building. Pete idly wondered if Julie could see them from the window of her office, but mostly his mind was concentrated on his growing distaste for what he was doing. He never should have become an undercover cop, he thought fretfully. The job required no conscience.

They neared the field house. The platinum blonde pointed to a stone bench just this side of it and said, "There's the bench I sat on that night. I walked clear up here in the dark, sat there all by myself and cried my eyes out."

There was no logical reason for it, but Pete found himself implicitly believing her. Suddenly he was convinced that, despite Bud Dutton's suspicion that Barbara's hysterics over Scooter Miller's death had been faked, she had been seated on this bench instead of lurking behind another one at the opposite end of the campus, and that he was badgering an innocent girl. All at once, he couldn't bring himself to pry into her grief anymore.

"We'd better start back," he said abruptly. "I'm supposed to meet Linc at the men's dorm."

Giving him a surprised look, she obediently turned to start back the other way.

Back at the girls' dorm, she burdened his conscience a little more by sincerely thanking him for taking her out of the dorm for a while.

"Just that little walk cheered me up a lot," she said. "I think it did me a world of good."

He muttered a vague promise to drop by to cheer her up again, and broke away.

When Linc came in an hour later, Pete was lying on his bed. Closing the door behind him and also closing the open bathroom door, Linc went over to sit on the edge of his own bed.

"I've been spending the afternoon worming my way into Dewey Stockton's confidence," the black youth said with distaste.

"I've been doing the same thing with Barbara Fenton," Pete told him. "And it left just as bad a taste in my mouth."

"Why don't we get out of this dirty racket?" Linc inquired.

Pete shrugged. "Maybe we're oversensitive. The captain says murderers don't deserve fair play."

"Both of them can't be the killer," Linc pointed out. "So any way you look at it, one of us shapes up as a rat."

"I'm only an ex-rat," Pete informed him. "I've decided I'm not going to romance that girl just to get her to bare her secrets."

"Well now, that's no more noble than my decision. I've decided I'm not going to play the buddy-buddy game with Dewey anymore."

They looked at each other, and suddenly both broke into grins.

"I don't think we have to worry about staying in this dirty racket," Pete said. "Probably we're both going to get fired."

When it neared 5 P.M. Pete and Linc decided to run over to the athletic administration building to confer with Julie, before she left for the day. They walked the distance and got there about five minutes of five. Julie was on the phone when they entered the office.

"Here they are now," she announced into the phone, then extended it to Pete. "Captain Greer," she said. "He phoned here, because he couldn't get you at the men's dorm."

"Yes, Captain?" Pete said into the phone.

"There's been a funny development, Pete," Captain Greer said. "Martinez and Bidder have left for the day, or I'd have them check it out. I guess you and Linc are elected."

"Okay. What's the development?"

"As you know, we have A.P.B.s out on Dinny Cord and Eddie Kye, including descriptions and license numbers of their cars. Well, about half an hour ago a cruising patrol car spotted Eddie Kye's automobile parked in the alley behind his apartment house. When the cops radioed in, I was immediately informed. It looked to me as though Eddie had taken a chance of sneaking back to his own place, figuring that's the last place we'd look for him, and had parked in the alley just in case there was a stakeout covering the front. So I ordered the patrol car cops to move in and arrest him. Their report just came back that no one answers the door, but that inside the apartment they can hear a record player with a cracked record on it playing the same refrain over and over. I ordered them to stand by until plainclothesmen got there."

"And that's us, huh?" Pete said. "What do you want us to do when we get there?"

"Get hold of the building manager and have him let you in the apartment."

"You think Eddie's holed up there and just refuses to answer the door?" Pete asked.

"He would reject that cracked record if he were able to," Adam Greer said testily.

After a moment of silence, Pete ventured, "You think he's dead?"

"I haven't the slightest idea, which is why I'm dispatching you and Linc to investigate. But it occurred to me that Dinny Cord has no way of knowing we're aware he's behind the bribery racket. Eddie was the only one you guys dealt with. Maybe Dinny figured that if Eddie went bye-bye, no one could ever tie him to the racket. On the other hand, Kye may simply have run home to pack, guessed that his car was being looked for and abandoned it in favor of taking a taxi to wherever he decided to hide out."

"Yes, sir," Pete said. "We'll check it out."

"I won't be here when you report back," the captain said. "You can contact me at home, though."

"All right, Captain," Pete said. "We'll let you know what we find out."

CHAPTER 21

HANGING up, Pete explained the situation to Linc and Julie. When he finished, he said to Julie, "Do you have to check out or something?"

She shook her head. "Mr. Doyle went home at four thirty." Removing her handbag from a bottom desk drawer, she said, "I'm all ready."

It was a few minutes' walk from the athletic administration building to where the Woody was parked on the dormitory parking lot. It was also a good distance from the college to Eighth and Hoover. It was almost five thirty when they arrived.

A police officer was sitting in a radio car in front. Pete showed the man his I.D. and explained that they had been sent by Captain Greer.

"Inside, apartment 204," the officer said. "My partner's standing by there."

Inside they climbed stairs to the second floor. Another uniformed officer was standing in front of apartment 204. Either none of the tenants of other apartments were as yet home from work or they were remarkably uncurious, because no one else was in the hall, and no doors were open.

Pete again showed his I.D. and announced that they had been sent by Captain Greer.

Jerking a thumb at the door numbered 204, the policeman said, "You can hear the record player, if you put your ear against the door. It isn't loud enough, otherwise."

Pete and Linc both went over to press their ears against the door. Faintly but clearly they could hear the voice of Nat King Cole singing over and over, "because it's you . . . because it's you . . . because it's you . . ."

Raising his head, Pete said to the uniformed man, "Okay, we can take over, now."

"You don't want me and my partner to stick around until you see what the situation is?" the man asked, surprised.

"It won't be necessary."

"Well, okay," the man said dubiously. "I think the manager's office is downstairs, if you want a passkey."

"We'll find it," Pete said, taking his shoulder and steering him toward the stairs.

When the policeman had disappeared downstairs, Linc said with a slight smile, "You don't want any witnesses to see that you're not going to quite follow the captain's orders, huh?"

"Why bother the apartment manager?" Pete inquired as he took a picklock from his pocket. "He may be the stuffy kind who would insist on a search warrant."

It took Pete only a couple of expert twists to open the door. He thrust in his head and looked around, going the rest of the way in only when he was satisfied that the front room was empty. Linc and Julie followed him inside.

The apartment was furnished with modern American furniture of average quality. The cracked record was playing on a combination radio-phonograph setting against the near wall. As Linc pushed the door shut behind them, Pete switched off the record player.

An archway across from the entrance led into a central hall off which could be seen the open doors to a bedroom and a bathroom. To the right, a similar archway led into a kitchen area.

Pete was heading for the archway across from the entrance, when he came to a dead halt and stared into the kitchen. Linc and Julie both went over to see what he was looking at.

Eddie Kye, in shirt sleeves, lay flat on his back on the floor next to a breakfast bar with three stools in front of it. The round wooden haft of an ordinary ice pick protruded from a spot directly over his heart.

Julie turned away and went over to sink onto a sofa

in the front room. Pete and Linc went into the kitchen and bent over the body.

Pete briefly touched the forehead, then raised the right arm and let it fall again.

"Rigor mortis has completely disappeared," he said. "It must have happened at least twenty-four hours ago."

Both rose to their feet. With Pete in the lead, they moved into the central hallway and glanced into the empty bathroom and bedroom. They came out into the front room again and looked at Julie.

"You all right?" Pete asked.

"Of course," she said, giving him a weak smile. "I just don't want to look at him unless I have to."

"No necessity," he told her. To Linc he said, "You see a phone anywhere?"

"On the kitchen wall," Linc said, gesturing that way.

Pete started in that direction, but stopped to stare at the front door as it slowly began to open. Both Linc and Julie stared at it, too.

When the door had swung all the way open, a short, stocky, balding man was revealed. Despite being clad in an expensive business suit instead of the greenish-gray uniform, which was the only thing Pete and Linc had previously seen him in, neither had any trouble recognizing the newcomer. It was the laundry-and-cleaning deliveryman, Johnny Merlin.

He looked familiar to Julie, too, because she had seen his mug shots the day they reviewed his record, but she couldn't place where she had seen him. She gazed at him with puzzled half-recognition.

Johnny Merlin's eyes narrowed. Moving inside, he closed the door behind him and looked from one to the other. He showed no recognition when he looked at Julie, which wasn't surprising since he had never seen her before, but Pete and Linc seemed to ring bells.

After studying them for a few seconds, he said, "Hey, don't you kids live in the men's dorm at Baldwin Hills College?"

Linc nodded, and Pete said, "Uh-huh."

"What you doing here?"

Pete jerked his head toward the kitchen. Merlin moved far enough into the room to see through the archway. His reaction, when he saw the dead man, was as unexpected as it was fast. His right hand streaked inside his coat under his left armpit and came out again gripping a thirty-eight automatic.

"Up," he ordered. "Get them real high."

Pete and Linc obediently elevated their hands. Julie delayed, until he snapped at her. "You too, babe!" Then she released her grip on the purse in her lap and raised her hands.

The stocky man circled around Pete and Linc, backed into the kitchen until he was alongside of the body, and looked down at it.

Pete said, "You've got the wrong slant, mister. We didn't make that hole in Eddie. If you look close, you'll see he's been dead quite a while."

"How do I know how long you've been here?" Merlin inquired.

Linc said, "Aw, come on, Merlin. We're here to investigate what killed him."

"What do you mean, investigate?" the man with the gun asked sharply. "And how do you know my name?"

Pete said, "If you'll let us put our hands down, we'll show you our I.D.s. We're cops."

Johnny Merlin stared at him without saying anything for some time, then looked at Linc and finally at Julie.

"All three of you?" he eventually asked.

"All three of us," Linc confirmed.

He started to lower his hands, then quickly raised them again when the stocky man snapped, "Keep them up!"

Julie said to Pete, "Who is this man? He looks familiar, but I can't place him."

"Johnny Merlin," Pete said. "You saw his mug shots."

Merlin's eyes slit. He came back out into the front room, cautiously keeping Pete and Linc covered as he circled around them.

"You people been looking over my record, huh?" he said. "Why are you two living in the men's dorm anyway, pretending to be students?"

Then his eyes widened again, and he answered his own question. "Hey, you're the cops Din—a fellow I know was telling me about getting to Eddie. I thought he was talking about those two jokers who picked me up and made me come up with an alibi for Wednesday night."

"Mike Martinez and Lee Bidder," Pete said.

"Yeah, they're the ones. But Din—the guy who told me a pair of cops had gotten to Eddie wasn't talking about them, was he? He meant you."

Pete said, "You're probably right. Didn't he tell you our names?"

Merlin shook his head. "What are your names?"

"I'm Pete Cochrane, my buddy is Linc Hayes and she's Julie Barnes."

"Can't say I'm glad to meet you," the stocky man sniffed. "This guy I mentioned seemed to think Eddie was as far as you got, but you must have me tied into it, too, or you wouldn't have been checking my record."

"We know you're the runner in the operation," Pete said.

"Yeah? What else you know?"

Linc said, "We know that the man whose name you've been rather clumsily trying to avoid mentioning is boss of the operation. Dinny Cord."

Merlin pursed his lips. "Well, now, that changes the picture a little. You two guys put your hands on top of your heads and turn your backs. Quick now!"

When both had complied, the stocky man gave each a quick but thorough shakedown. He looked surprised at finding no weapons.

"What kind of cops are you that don't carry guns?" he inquired.

When neither answered, Merlin went over and lifted Julie's purse from her lap. He gave it a quick search, pausing to study her I.D., then tossed it back in her lap when he found it weaponless. Running his gaze up and down her slim figure, he decided there was no place a gun could be concealed in her miniskirted dress.

"Okay, you can all put your hands down," he said.

Julie dropped her hands into her lap. Pete and Linc lowered theirs and turned to face the man with the gun.

"Why don't you put that thing away, now?" Pete suggested.

"I haven't decided what to do with you people, yet."

Linc said, "There isn't much you can do with three cops that won't get you in a barrel of trouble."

"I think I'm already in a barrel of it," Merlin said. "Shut up, while I think."

Linc, Pete and Julie all remained silent while he thought. After a time, he came to a decision.

"Guess I better just take you to Dinny and let him decide," he announced.

Linc gave Pete a bitter look. "You and your easy way to do things," he said. "If you hadn't shooed off those two cops, this joker would never have taken us."

"What two cops?" Merlin asked sharply.

Pete said, "The ones covering the front and back of this building, waiting for us to come out."

After staring at him for a moment, Johnny Merlin smiled without humor. "You're trying to make a funny. Your partner said you shooed them off. I figure he's talking about some cops who were standing by, waiting for you to get here, and you dismissed them."

"Figure what you please," Pete said with a shrug. "But don't say I didn't warn you, when you take us out of here under that gun, and you get a bullet in your fat brain."

"I guess I'll chance it," Merlin said. "Did you say your name was Pete Cochrane?"

"Yes."

"Okay, Cochrane, you're going first. You're next in line, Hayes." He motioned Julie to her feet with his gun. "And you're last, baby. Now you two guys get this straight. If there are any cops out there, and they start shooting, this lady cop gets a slug right in the spine, because I'm going to be just one step behind her. The same thing goes if either of you make any kind of break. Understand?"

Julie paled. Pete and Linc each gave her reassuring smiles.

"We understand," Pete said. "There aren't really any cops outside, and we won't make any breaks. So don't get trigger happy."

"That's better," Merlin said in a satisfied voice. "Let's get moving."

CHAPTER 22

JOHNNY MERLIN backed to the door, opened it and glanced over his shoulder into the hall. Then he stepped aside and motioned with his gun for Pete to begin the parade.

"Turn right, because we're going down the back stairs," he instructed as Pete went by.

When Linc, then Julie had followed Pete through the door, the stocky man thrust the gun into his coat pocket, but kept it trained on Julie's back through the cloth. They met no one in the hallway or on the rear stairs. The stairs ended at a back door, which led out into a narrow yard enclosed by a six-foot-high board fence.

Merlin ordered his three captives to halt and stand aside, while he cracked open the back gate and peered into the alley. Satisfied that it was deserted, he pulled it open the rest of the way and motioned the trio through it.

Pulled over close to the fence in order to allow room for other cars to pass were two parked cars. Pete and Linc recognized the front one as the same Ford Eddie Kye had been driving, when they followed him from Bertie's Bar and Grill to West Los Angeles. Behind it was a dark-green four-door Oldsmobile sedan.

Merlin ordered Pete and Linc to get in front. The car was parked so close to the wooden fence that only the doors on its left side could be opened. Linc slid beneath the wheel over to the right, Pete took the driver's seat.

Merlin opened the rear door, had Julie get in and took the gun from his pocket again before getting in next to her.

"Same rule as before holds," he announced. "You guys act up, and the lady cop gets shot. Okay?"

Linc said with an edge to his voice, "We already told you we'd behave, Merlin. Just don't get nervous."

Johnny Merlin tossed a set of car keys over Pete's shoulder to land in his lap.

"Take Eighth Street west to the Harbor Freeway," he instructed. "Take the freeway south."

Pete started the car, backed to pull around the Ford parked in front of them and drove to the mouth of the alley. He circled back to Eighth Street, turned west on it as instructed, and a few blocks later drove onto the Harbor Freeway.

As they pulled out of the acceleration lane and Pete drove the speed to its legal limit of sixty-five, he inquired conversationally, "How'd you happen to drop in on Eddie when you did, Merlin?"

After considering this question, apparently their captor decided there would be no harm in answering it. "Dinny sent me."

"Oh? For what?"

"To find out what was holding Eddie up. He was supposed to come to the same place we're going, but he never showed. Dinny expected him early yesterday morning, around 5 or 6 A.M."

Linc said, "Why that particular hour?"

"Well, as I get it, Eddie wanted to go back to his joint to pick up some bread and pack some rags, in case he and Dinny were going to have to hide out for a long time. He figured the place might be staked out, but along toward morning the cops would start to give up on him, and at most there would probably only be a stakeout posted in front by then. If he waited until about 3 or 4 A.M., then parked in the alley and sneaked in the back way, he figured he had a good chance to get in, pick up what he needed and get out again without being spotted. So he told Dinny he would hole up in some motel until early morning, then scoot by his place to get his rags and some money, before joining Dinny at the cottage. It only takes about an hour to get to the cottage, so Eddie should have been there by 6 A.M. Thursday at the latest."

"Where is this cottage?" Pete inquired.

"You'll find out. Take the Manchester Avenue off-ramp and head west on Manchester."

Pete did as directed. They stayed on Manchester Avenue clear through Inglewood and Westchester, then Merlin ordered Pete to take Alternate 101 north.

They passed through Santa Monica to the point where Alternate 101 became the Pacific Coast Highway and continued north.

Although sections of it are divided road, the Pacific Coast Highway is not a freeway. It passes through numerous coastal resort towns, where the posted speed limit drops to as low as thirty-five miles an hour. If Julie hadn't been with them Pete might have deliberately failed to slow down when they passed through these reduced speed zones, in the hope of being flagged down by a police car. But he was unwilling to take any chances at all with her safety. He scrupulously obeyed all traffic laws.

They continued north on the highway for nearly an hour. By then, dusk was falling and Pete switched on the headlights.

There had been no conversation for a long time. But just as Pete turned on the headlights, Johnny Merlin broke the silence by saying, "There's a road that angles off to the left just ahead. Take it."

As they swung onto the road, Pete noted a street sign designating it as Hueneme Road. Shortly afterward, Merlin had them turn left again onto a narrow, unmarked road leading to the ocean. At its end, he directed Pete to pull into the driveway of an isolated beach cottage, situated only about fifty yards from the water.

Pete cut the engine and lights, and they all got out. The three members of the Mod Squad looked around, Pete and Linc with curiosity, Julie more with trepidation. There was still enough light to make out the surrounding area dimly.

Pete was fairly familiar with this area, because he had surfed off a number of the beaches along here. They were only a mile or two east of the town of Port Hueneme, he realized.

The Pacific coast curved to the west along here, so that the ocean was due south of both Port Hueneme and this beach instead of being west, as is normal along most of the coast. A line of sand dunes blocked the view to the north. Only two other cottages were visible to the east, one about a hundred yards away, the other some fifty yards beyond that. Both were unlighted, and perhaps were boarded up for the winter, although light was now failing too fast to make that out at that distance. To the west, there was nothing but sand.

In the water in front of the cottage was a single boat slip on pontoons with what appeared to be about an eighteen-foot power boat tied to it.

Good place for a hideout, Pete thought dourly. Only two neighbors within viewing distance, and neither appeared to be in residence.

The cottage was a white frame building of one story; with an attached garage. At first glance it too appeared to be unlighted, but then vertical cracks of light centering a couple of windows made Pete, Linc and Julie realize that opaque drapes were drawn over them.

Johnny Merlin herded them toward the cottage. The door opened as they approached, and a tall, skeletal man in his fifties, with a full head of curling gray hair, peered out at them. Although none of the Mod Squad had ever seen him in person before, from having viewed his mug shots they recognized the beaked nose and piercing black eyes as those of Dinsmore (Dinny) Cord.

"What in the devil is this?" Cord demanded in a strangely high-pitched voice, when he saw that Merlin was covering the three young strangers with a gun.

"Tell you inside," the stocky man informed him.

Dinny Cord backed out of the doorway to let the others in. The door led into a large room running the width of this end of the house and serving as a combination kitchen-and-dining area and living room. The kitchen equipment was modern enough, but the rest of the furniture had the cast-off look common to beach cottage furnishings.

Across from the door by which they had entered was a hallway running to another door facing the beach. Four doors off this hallway, two on either side, could be seen.

As the stocky Merlin closed the door behind him, Dinny Cord glared from the three captives to the gun in Merlin's hand, and said in his high-pitched voice, "Well?"

"They was at Eddie's place," Merlin said. "Eddie's lying on his back on his kitchen floor with an ice pick in him. Looks like he's been dead for quite a while.

Cord's piercing eyes became slits. "Eddie's dead?" He looked at the three members of the Mod Squad again. "These kids did it?"

"Oh, no. They was there investigating the thing."

Dinny Cord stared at his hatchet man for a long time, before finally squeaking, "You mean they're cops?"

"These two guys are the same ones that got to Eddie," Merlin explained. "The white guy is named Pete Cochrane, and the black guy is Linc Hayes. The lady cop's name I forget." He looked at Julie and said, "What's your name again, baby?"

"Julie Barnes," she said meekly.

"Are you crazy, bringing cops here?" the loan-shark-racketeer yelled.

"They already knew all about you heading up the Baldwin Hills College deal," Merlin said in a reasonable tone. "Also that I was your runner. So bringing them here didn't tip them to anything they haven't already got."

"Except where I'm hiding out!" Cord screeched at him. "Why didn't you just lose them? What am I supposed to do with them here?"

"Well, I don't know, boss," the stocky man said, scratching his balding head without letting his gun droop or taking his attention from the three under it. "You always say for me not to try to do any thinking, so I figured you'd want to decide what to do about them. How did I know you wouldn't get sore if I didn't bring them in?"

After gazing at his subordinate for several seconds, Cord turned his hands palm up in a helpless gesture. "You sure followed my advice by not thinking," he said with sudden weariness. "What you've pulled is a triple kidnapping, which could get both of us thirty years."

Cord swung his attention to the captives. "Was he telling the truth before?" he asked generally. "Did you people already have me made as director of the Baldwin Hills College thing before Johnny stumbled into you?"

Pete said, "There's been an A.P.B. out on you ever since you shook your tail Wednesday afternoon, Dinny. You must have known we had you made or you wouldn't have gone through all those fancy maneuvers to get rid of your tail."

"I didn't know for sure I was staked out," Cord said. "I just wasn't taking any chances." He turned back to Johnny Merlin. "Now that you've brought them here, there isn't much we can do, except get rid of them permanently."

Julie paled. Linc and Pete regarded the man with disbelief.

Linc said, "Seems to me both you and Merlin are overreacting, Cord. It's pretty apparent neither of you hit Eddie Kye, or even know who did. Did you have anything to do with Scooter Miller's murder?"

Cord said impatiently, "I didn't even know the kid was dead, until I heard it on the radio at noon yesterday. And you must know the cops checked out Johnny and cleared him."

"Then why are you pushing the panic button? You could both get life at the very least for rubbing three cops, but what can you get for the Baldwin Hills caper?"

"Death," the cadaverous Cord said.

Linc regarded him quizzically. "How you figure that?"

"I've been taking the bookies around town real good on that setup, buddy. On top of what I booked myself, I've burnt them for close to 500 G's. You know who bankrolls the bookies in L.A.?"

Linc said, "Oh," and looked at Pete.

Pete had no trouble understanding what Dinny Cord meant, either. If the Mafia ever found out that the loan-shark had taken it for a half million dollars on fixed games, he was as good as dead. Cord couldn't afford to stop at anything to prevent news of the racket from being made public, or at least to prevent his connection with it from becoming known.

Even the murder of three police officers.

CHAPTER 23

DINNY CORD said to Merlin, "We won't be able to do anything, until it gets good and dark. Meanwhile we'd better tie them up."

He rummaged in a kitchen cabinet drawer and found a coil of clothesline. While Johnny Merlin kept the three captives covered, Cord bound their hands behind them, cutting the line into the lengths he wanted with a pair of scissors he took from another drawer. Then he ordered them to sit in the living-room portion of the room.

Julie and Pete chose a sagging sofa to sit on. Linc took an aged easy chair. None could sit very comfortably with their hands bound behind them.

As soon as they were safely tied up, the stocky man had put away his gun. He said to Dinny Cord, "Can we have some supper, while we're waiting?"

Cord, who apparently was the cook, began preparing a meal of hamburger patties, fried potatoes and canned peas. He made only enough for himself and Merlin, and they ate it in front of the three prisoners. Obviously, Cord felt it was unnecessary to feed guests who weren't going to live long enough to digest.

While the pair was eating, Julie whispered to Pete, "What do you think they're going to do?"

She had become quite pale, he noted. He gave her an encouraging smile and said in a low voice, "Nothing, probably. When Dinny starts thinking it over, he ought to realize this is stupid."

The words didn't cheer her much, mainly because she knew they were designed to do just that and that Pete didn't believe them himself. The after-dinner conversation of their captors was eyen less cheering.

Dinny Cord had washed dishes, and Johnny Merlin

had dried them. As Merlin hung up the towel, Cord glanced at a wall clock and said, "Eight o'clock. It'll be plenty late by the time we get the boat loaded."

"Loaded with what?" Merlin asked.

"There's a set of tire chains in the trunk of my car in the garage. They ought to be enough weight for the two guys. There's also an extra boat anchor in the garage that we can use for the girl."

"Okay," Merlin said. "Give me your car keys."

Cord produced keys from the pocket and handed them over. "Better leave your gun with me while you're gone," he said. "I'm not carrying one."

This was obvious, since the man was in shirt sleeves. Merlin produced his thirty-eight automatic and offered it butt first. Cord thrust it into his belt.

Johnny Merlin went out, and a few moments later they could hear the creaks of heavy springs as the garage overhead door was raised.

Pete said, "You really going to stick your neck out this far, Dinny? If you turned us loose, we might be willing to forget the kidnapping charge, so all you'd face over the Baldwin Hills thing would be conspiracy to defraud, bribery and bookmaking."

"Plus the Freak."

All three members of the Mod Squad knew what he meant by this, because every member on the LAPD knew who the Freak was. Cord was referring to Luigi (the Freak) Cellino, reputed head of Southern California's Cosa Nostra family.

As Pete couldn't think of any arguments strong enough to overcome the skinny man's fear of the Mafia, he shut up and threw the ball to Linc by giving him an inquiring look.

Linc couldn't think of any arguments, either.

Since the boys knew that simply pleading for their lives would do no good, even if they had been willing to stoop to it, neither of them made any further attempt to reason with Cord. Julie looked from one to the other, realized they had given up and became even paler than she already was.

In about ten minutes, Johnny Merlin came back in and announced that the boat was loaded. Dinny Cord gave him back his pistol, and Merlin put it away.

Cord lifted a cloth fishing jacket from a wall hook and shrugged into it. He picked up the remnant of the clothesline he had used to tie up Pete, Linc and Julie, presumably taking it along to bind the tire chains and the boat anchor to the bodies of the three victims, before they were tossed overboard.

"Let's go," he said to Merlin.

"You want me to burn them now?" the stocky man inquired.

The cadaverous Cord gave him a pained look. "And then have to drag all that dead weight fifty yards? Not to mention bloodying up the cottage. Why burn them at all, when the ocean will take care of things?"

"Well, I was just asking," the gunman said defensively.

Pete said in a disgusted voice, "No wonder you've been busted so many times, Merlin. You're stupid."

The stocky man looked at him, then snickered. "Not stupid enough to go swimming with a tire chain wrapped around my neck, buddy."

Dinny Cord regarded his subordinate with mild surprise. "Well, well, you actually managed a comeback, Johnny. I'm proud of you." He turned to the three prisoners. "On your feet, all of you."

Linc said to Pete, "Why make it easy for them? Let's make them drag us."

Cord said almost casually to Merlin, "Shoot the girl."

Merlin was reaching under his arm, when both Pete and Linc bounced to their feet.

"Whoa!" Linc said. "We're going to cooperate real nice."

"Then start moving," Cord said coldly, jerking a thumb in the direction of the door that gave onto the beach.

He moved ahead of them to open the door. Linc followed, then Pete. Julie got to her feet and followed Pete on unsteady legs. Johnny Merlin took his hand from under his coat and came last.

It was a bright moonlit night, and the ocean was relatively calm, with only slight swells. The beach sloped steeply enough at the water's edge so that the tide didn't move in and out any appreciable distance, and a narrow wooden ramp led from above the high-tide mark to the floating boat slip. Dinny Cord led the way down the ramp.

The eighteen-foot boat was powered with twin seventy-five horsepower outboard motors, with front-seat controls. There was only a single two-passenger seat, the entire area behind it being open. Dinny Cord didn't keep a very taut ship, because the deck of the stern area was littered with life jackets, fishing equipment, oars, and the recently-added tire chains and spare boat anchor.

Cord tossed the coil of clothesline in with the other litter and directed the bound captives to get in back. Linc stepped in first, moving awkwardly because of his tied hands, and settled on the port side just behind the front seat.

Pete was next, and chose the starboard side directly across from Linc. A slight swell raised the boat a few inches just as he prepared to sit, causing him to lose his balance and come down more suddenly than he intended. He sat hard on the edge of some kind of rectangular metal box about a foot high, then slid off it, painfully scraping his lower back against one corner of the box as he settled to a seated position on the deck. The box continued to stick into his back uncomfortably.

Julie got in, considerably more gracefully then either Linc or Pete, and sat aft alongside of Pete.

Dinny Cord stepped into the forward seat, slid behind the wheel, started the engines and switched on running lights.

"Cast off," he called.

Johnny Merlin loosened the lines, tossed them aboard and jumped in back. He seated himself aft on the port side, next to Linc.

The boat backed from the slip, swung around and headed out to sea. Cord maintained a moderate speed. Probably the powerful twin engines would have driven a boat that size along at fifty miles an hour, but he kept it throttled down to about twenty, apparently because it rode the waves most easily at that speed.

Cord headed in a southwesterly direction, as that was the quickest route to deep water along this particular stretch of coast. The air was a bit crisp, but not unpleasantly cool, the sea was moderate and moonlight made for excellent visibility. It could have been an enjoyable trip under other circumstances.

Pete grew conscious of his hand touching a small handle behind his back. He had already decided that the box he was leaning against was a fishing tackle box, and now he cautiously felt to see if he could figure out how it was constructed. After feeling it all over, he decided that it contained two drawers that slid out horizontally. The upper was only about two inches deep, and the lower one was a good eight inches deep.

After a little experimentation, he deduced that a button on top of the handle of each drawer had to be depressed to release a catch before the drawer could be pulled open.

Unfortunately the drawers opened in Pete's direction instead of to one side or the other, and his back was pressed against them. As unobtrusively as possible, he inched himself forward so as to leave a gap between his back and the tackle box.

He had shifted only about three inches away from the box when Johnny Merlin leaned forward and peered at him. Pete's heart climbed to his throat, and he sat completely still.

After a long moment the stocky man switched his gaze to Julie, then peered sideways at Linc. He was just routinely keeping his eye on all three prisoners, Pete realized with relief.

He shifted himself forward again, a fraction of an inch at a time, until his back was about six inches from the box.

Pete owned a tackle box himself, but of different construction than this one. His had a lid that, when opened, made a shallow tray, connected to the lid by jointed steel strips, rise out of the box and slide back over the open lid. Below the shallow tray was a much deeper compartment.

Although the construction of the two boxes was different, Pete assumed, from the arrangement of equipment inside his, that the narrow upper drawer of this one would probably contain nothing but lures, hooks, sinkers and other small items of that nature. Larger items—such as a fishing knife—should be in the lower drawer.

The twin engines made too much noise for him to have to worry about either Merlin or Cord hearing him rummaging through the contents of the tackle box. Pulling the lower drawer open until it pressed into his back, he groped inside it.

He felt several spools of wire leader, what felt like a fish stringer, a scaler and a number of plastic boxes that might have contained anything. Then, clear at the bottom of the drawer, his fingers touched a leather sheath, and his heart jumped.

Cautiously, he worked the sheathed fishing knife up through the welter of other items until it was clear of the drawer, then leaned back to press the drawer closed. Gripping the sheath with his left hand, he worked the knife from it with his right. By its feel he guessed that the thick blade was about six inches long.

Gingerly, he touched a thumb to the cutting edge. His caution wasn't necessary. Apparently, Dinny Cord took no better care of his fishing equipment than he did of his boat. The knife was so dull, he could press his thumb against it firmly without drawing blood.

It is awkward enough to cut your own bonds with a sharp knife when your hands are tied behind you. With a dull one it is just barely possible. Pete sawed away without making very appreciable headway.

Meanwhile, they were now far enough out to sea so that the shoreline could no longer be seen in the moonlight, although the lights of Port Hueneme still could. Sailing along at a steady twenty-mile-an-hour clip, they could make five miles in fifteen minutes, and Pete guessed they had been moving out to sea at least that long.

He had managed to cut about halfway through the rope, when Dinny Cord throttled the engines down to idle, shifted into neutral and let the boat drift. The lights of an off-shore oil rig could be seen a couple of miles to the northwest, but no boat lights were visible in any direction. They were alone miles from shore.

Cord said, "This should be far out enough."

Johnny Merlin climbed to his feet, then stooped to pick up one of the tire chains and the coil of clothesline.

"You should have brought the scissors," he said to Cord. "How am I going to cut this?"

Turning around in the seat, Cord pointed to where Pete was sitting and said, "There's a knife in the bait box behind him."

Pete was desperately sawing with the dull knife. Merlin looked down at him, saw the tense expression on his face and caught the slight, rhythmic movement of his shoulders caused by working the knife blade up and down. Instantly realizing what was happening, the stocky man dropped the chain and the coil of rope, fell into a crouch, and his right hand streaked toward his armpit.

CHAPTER 24

THE clothesline binding Pete's wrists was sawed through only about three-fourths of the way. Dropping the knife, Pete gave a mighty jerk and the remaining strands snapped.

Even as his hands broke free, he knew he was too late, though. Merlin's automatic had cleared its holster and was swinging to level at his chest. Pete braced himself against the expected bullet.

Merlin was crouched in the center of the boat, half-way between Linc and Pete. His crouching position offered too inviting a target for Linc to pass up. Sliding forward until he was flat on his back, Linc brought his knees up to his chest, then drove the soles of both feet against the seat of the gunman's pants with pile-driver force.

Johnny Merlin probably weighed 185 pounds, but the force of the two-footed kick lifed him completely into the air. He arched right over Pete's head, dropping the gun in order to have both hands free for a desperate grab at Pete's shoulders.

He missed and belly flopped into the water with an

enormous splash, which rained spray on everyone in the boat.

Dinny Cord bounced to his knees on the forward seat and leaned over the back of the seat to reach for the dropped gun. Pete got to it first. He placed the muzzle about an inch from Cord's beaked nose.

"Just turn around again and face forward, Dinny," Pete said. "Then I won't have to shorten your nose a couple of inches."

Dinny stared at him without moving for several seconds, his reaching arm still extended over the back of the seat. Then he sighed, swiveled around and slid behind the wheel again.

Johnny Merlin had threshed his way to the side of the boat and was hanging on, coughing and sputtering.

"Help!" he squealed. "I can't swim."

"How'd you make it back to the boat, then?" Pete inquired.

"Help!" the man in the water repeated. "Don't let me drown."

"You won't drown," Pete said disgustedly. "I'll get to you in a minute."

Linc rolled over on his stomach as Pete stuck the gun in his belt and picked up the fish knife. With both hands free, the dull blade proved more effective. It took Pete only a few minutes to saw through Linc's bonds.

He cut Julie's also, before going to Merlin's rescue. Then he sheathed the knife and put it back in the tackle box. Only after handing the gun to Linc did he lean over the side and offer a helping hand to the man in the water. Merlin eagerly gripped the offered right hand with his own right.

Pete said, "Julie, you and Linc both sit on the opposite gunwale so the boat doesn't tip when I pull him in. But mind you don't fall overboard when it rolls that way."

Both sat on the gunwale, and Linc put his arm behind Julie's back to grip the gunwale beyond her and keep her from doing what Pete had warned her against. With his left hand, Pete gripped the wrist of the hand he was holding with his right, straightened up, braced one foot against the gunwale and heaved Johnny Merlin over the side into the boat. The boat rocked back and forth, but not too badly because the moment Merlin came over the boat, Linc dropped to his knees inside the boat, pulling Julie with him, to shift the center of the gravity back where it belonged.

Merlin remained on hands and knees for a few moments, dripping saltwater on the deck, then crawled over to his former position and collapsed with his back against the side of the boat. Linc resumed his former place, too, crossed his ankles and rested the butt of the automatic on his right knee. Pete and Julie moved back into their old places.

"Okay, Dinny, you can head in again," Pete said. "And this time, open it up. We haven't had any dinner."

Back at the cottage, they allowed Johnny Merlin time to change into dry clothing. Then they drove into town in Merlin's Oldsmobile. Pete drove, with Julie sitting next to him. Linc sat in back on the right side, with Dinny Cord between him and Merlin. Since the Mod Squad wasn't in the habit of carrying handcuffs, Linc kept the thirty-eight automatic trained on them.

The only conversation on the way in was when Julie said to Pete, "Didn't you mention something about dinner?"

Pete smiled at her. "An hour ago, you didn't look like you had any appetite."

"An hour ago I didn't, but I do, now."

"After we book the suspects, we'll go get a giant pizza," Pete told her.

It was 10:30 P.M. when Pete drove the Oldsmobile into the Police Building garage. The attendant came over and said, "Hey, this is no police car."

"Belongs to him," Pete said, jerking a thumb over his shoulder at Merlin. "He won't be going anywhere for a long time, so stick it in impound until you get instructions."

The attendant glanced at Merlin and Cord without curiosity and said; "Okay."

The occupants of the car all got out, and the attendant climbed under the wheel. Linc gestured toward the elevator with the gun. The two suspects meekly moved in that direction. They all took the elevator to the third floor.

Night activity in the LAPD Homicide Division varies tremendously. Some nights they have so much work that they have to call members of the day watch back to duty. Other nights, they sit around and look at each other. This seemed to be one of the latter. No one was in the squad room; except Sergeant Bud Dutton and the rubelike Hank Looper. They sat on opposite sides of one of the long tables watching a portable television set.

When the Mod Squad herded the two arrestees into the squad room, Looper got up and switched off the television set. Both detectives regarded the gun in Linc's hand with some surprise.

"I thought you people never carried guns," Bud Dutton said.

"Only when we take them away from people," Linc told him. "This one belongs to him." He nodded toward Johnny Merlin; then slid the gun across the table to the black Homicide officer almost with relief.

Dutton released the ammunition clip, ejected the shell in the chamber and laid the gun, the clip and the loose shell on the table. Meanwhile, Hank Looper had returned to the table and stood looking at the two suspects without expression.

"Evening, Dinny," he said. "Hi, Johnny. What have you two been up to?"

"Don't ask them anything, yet," Linc said quickly. "They haven't been warned."

"They both been in here so many times, they ought to know it by heart by now," Dutton said. "But go ahead."

Linc said to Cord and Merlin, "You two are formally under arrest for kidnapping and attempted murder. You are not required to make a statement of any kind; and if you do speak, anything you say may be taken down and used against you in evidence. You are entitled to legal counsel, and if you can't afford a lawyer, one will be furnished you at public expense."

Dinny Cord said carefully, "I'll want to phone my lawyer before we're booked, but there's no rush. Johnny and I want to cooperate. I'm not planning to create any legal problems for you to wrestle with tonight, such as having my lawyer get some judge out of bed for writs of habeas corpus. We won't fuss about spending the night in jail. I just want to arrange for him to come down first thing in the morning."

Pete said with sour amusement, "You won't fuss because you know no judge would grant you writs, or even fix bail on the charges of kidnapping and the attempted murder of three police officers. Don't do us any favors, Dinny."

The skeletal Cord shrugged. Pulling a chair out from the table next to the one where Dutton was sitting, he swung it around to face the other table and sat in it. Johnny Merlin swung another around and sat next to him.

Julie decided to sit, too, and rounded the table to where Hank Looper was standing to take the chair he had formerly occupied on the opposite side of the table from Bud Dutton. Pete and Linc remained standing.

Lieutenant Wes Roberts, Homicide's night watch commander, came from his office at that moment. Roberts was a tall beanpole of a man, with a perpetually sad expression. After greeting Pete, Linc and Julie, he examined their two prisoners with morose curiosity.

"What's with them?" he inquired.

Pointing to the skinny man, Bud Dutton said, "This one is Dinny Cord. I'm sure you've heard of him. The other is just one of his minions, name of Johnny Merlin. Pete, Linc and Julie brought them in for kidnapping and attempted murder, but they haven't told us any details, yet."

Wes Roberts looked inquiringly at Pete and Linc. "The kidnapping and attempted murder of whom?"

"Us," Pete said. He pointed to Johnny Merlin. "He walked in on us at Eddie Kye's apartment at about 5:30 P.M., pulled a gun and forced all three of us to drive to a cottage Dinny owns near Port Hueneme. They had plans to drown us in the ocean, but we upset them."

Lieutenant Roberts frowned at the two suspects, then turned back to Pete. "What were you doing at Eddie Kye's apartment?"

"Looking at his body."

"His body?" Hank Looper said in a startled voice. "You mean Eddie's dead?"

"Uh-huh. For quite some time. I'd guess at least twenty-four hours even before we saw him. Somebody stuck an ice pick in him. From conversations between them, incidentally, it doesn't seem likely it was either of these guys."

"What's Kye's address?" Wes Roberts asked.

Pete said, "Apartment 204 of the Warwick at Eighth and Hoover."

Roberts wrote the address on a scratch pad lying on the table and tore off the sheet. "One of the Gang Squad cars is cruising in that area. I'll have them cover it. Hold the details about this kidnapping and attempted murder until I get back."

He returned to his office, and a moment later they could hear him issuing orders over the phone. When he came back out, Pete, with occasional embellishments from Linc and Julie, recounted in detail what had happened that evening.

When he finished, Lieutenant Roberts let his eyes glitter at the suspects. "We're not too fond of cop-killers around here," he announced. "Or even of would-be cop-killers. We can probably get you guys life in the Joint."

Both men were aware that the Joint was underworld jargon for San Quentin. Johnny Merlin licked his lips. Dinny Cord merely narrowed his eyes.

The latter said, "That sounds like a deal offer is coming."

"You know we don't make deals," Roberts said harshly. "But if we write 'cooperative' on a case record, the D.A. might take it into consideration in drawing up an indictment."

"I don't care how you phrase it," Cord said. "What's the proposition?"

"Just what I said. You cooperate and we'll put it on your record."

"Cooperate about what?"

"The Miller and Kye murders."

Dinny Cord shrugged his thin shoulders. "Since neither me nor Johnny had anything to do with them, we got nothing to lose. What do you want to know?"

Pete said, "Let's add your cooperation about the

Baldwin Hills caper, too. We want the names of every athlete at Baldwin Hills who accepted a bribe."

"Eddie handled all that," Cord said quickly. "I don't know any of the names."

"Aw, come on, Dinny," Linc said. "You weren't paying off without knowing who was getting the money."

"Honest, I don't know," Cord said in an earnest voice, then added helpfully, "Maybe Eddie kept some kind of records from which you could get the names, if you search his place."

Julie said, "He's not going to cooperate about the briberies. He's afraid of the Mafia."

"Yeah," Pete said. "Probably with good reason. Okay, Dinny, we'll settle for the straight goods on the Miller and Kye kills temporarily. You have any ideas about either?"

Cord shook his head. "They're as big a mystery to me as to you guys. I can tell you this, though. Young Scooter's hit had nothing to do with his arrangement with Eddie. When Eddie came to my place and told me that the last two athletes Scooter had steered to him were cops, my only reaction was for both of us to drop out of sight, until the heat died down. I didn't order the kid scratched."

"How about Eddie?" Linc asked. "Could he have pulled it on his own?"

"Not Eddie," the skinny man said in a definite tone. "He never did his own thinking, anymore than Johnny here does. He was strictly an order taker."

CHAPTER 25

Bud Dutton rose from his chair, went over to an evidence locker and returned with the familiar large manila envelope. He removed the knife that had killed Scooter Miller from it and showed it to Merlin and Cord.

"Either of you ever see this?" he inquired.

Johnny Merlin gave his head a sullen shake after a mere glance at the weapon. But Dinny Cord reached out to take the knife from the black officer's hand and examined it carefully.

When he handed it back, he said, "Eddie carried one exactly like it. I can't be sure that's it, though."

Julie said, "I thought you were sure Eddie couldn't have been Scooter's killer."

"Is that what killed the Miller kid?" Cord asked in surprise.

All six police officers examined him suspiciously, wondering if this was a put-on, but apparently the surprise was honest, because Cord was still gazing at the weapon, and now he looked puzzled.

He said, "It sure looks like Eddie's knife, but it wouldn't be like Eddie to pull anything as big as a murder on his own."

With a shrug, Bud Dutton returned the knife to its envelope. He went over and replaced the envelope in the evidence locker.

Pete said to Julie and Linc, "I don't think we can accomplish anything more tonight. Unless you want to wait for the report to come in on Eddie Kye."

Julie said reproachfully, "That might be hours."

"She's thinking about that pizza you promised," Linc said with a grin. "We can get briefed on Eddie just as well in the morning."

Pete said, "Okay, let's take these jokers down to the Felony Section and book them."

"I would like to contact my lawyer first," Dinny Cord reminded him.

Pete shrugged. On each of the tables were telephones spaced at intervals. Pete picked up the one nearest to the skinny man and said, "What's his number?"

When Dinny Cord gave him the number, Pete dialed for an outside line, relayed the number to the switchboard operator and handed the phone to Dinny.

From the conversation, it seemed apparent that the lawyer had been gotten out of bed. Cord kept his word about not creating any legal problems that night. He merely briefly explained the charges on which he and Johnny Merlin had been arrested, and asked the lawyer to come to the Felony Section in the Police Building the first thing in the morning.

When he hung up, Pete, Linc and Julie took the two men down to the Felony Section, had them booked and locked in cells for the night. From there they went to the dispatcher to arrange for transportation to Eighth and Hoover to pick up the Woody.

An empty patrol car and a morgue wagon were parked in front of the building containing Eddie Kye's apartment.

"Guess they haven't finished the investigation, yet," Pete said. "Shall we stop in to see how it's going?"

"You said it wouldn't matter if we waited until morning," Julie said plaintively.

Pete grinned at ther. "All right, hungry. We'll go get your pizza."

Neither Pete nor Linc had any Saturday classes, but they would have cut them even if they had. Julie didn't have to go to work on Saturday in the Athletic Department, either. At nine Saturday morning, the three of them arrived at Captain Greer's office.

After making their report, they headed for Homicide Division. It was about twenty after nine when they walked into the squad room.

There was always more activity on the Homicide day watch than on the night trick. A number of detectives were in the squad room, some working on reports, some questioning suspects or witnesses, others talking on telephones. Sergeant Mike Martinez and Officer Lee Bidder were seated side-by-side at a corner table, looking over a case record.

Both looked up as the trio came into the squad room. Martinez waved them over. Pete, Linc and Julie went over and took chairs on the opposite side of the table from the two detectives, Julie, as always, in the middle.

"Hear you people had quite a time last night," the handsome Martinez said with a grin.

"It was interesting while it lasted," Pete said. "Dinny's lawyer show, yet?"

"He's been and gone," Martinez said. "Announced he's going to try to get a bail hearing set. I don't think he's too confident of getting his clients released on bail, though. If it was just attempted murder, he could swing it, but kidnapping is a pretty tough rap."

Linc said, "Did the guys investigating the Eddie Kye murder turn anything interesting?"

"Not much. Lee and I were just going over the case record." The Mexican-American rapped his knuckles on the case folder between them. "Coroner's office fixes time of death as somewhere between 4 and 10 A.M. Thursday morning. He'd been dead too long to guess any closer. The ice-pick handle had been wiped clean. There was no sign of a struggle, no sign of forced entry, and the motive couldn't have been robbery because there was a wallet in his pocket containing eight hundred dollars. The boys figure he was punctured by somebody he knew and let in."

"Was there a switchblade knife on him?" Pete asked.

Martinez shook his head. "There's mention in the record that Wes Roberts asked them to check for one. Either Bill Carey or Joe Sull—the Gang Squad guys who had the case—must have phoned in to talk to Wes after you left last night. According to the record, they turned the place inside out. Not only was there no such knife on the body, there wasn't any in the apartment. The only weapon they found was a loaded revolver in a dresser drawer."

Pete, Linc and Julie all looked at each other. "Curiouser and curiouser, as Alice said," Pete commented. "It seems unlikely, but the evidence points more and more to Eddie slipping that knife in Scooter."

"Then who killed Eddie?" Julie asked.

Pete shrugged. "Maybe somebody avenging Scooter. Larry Coons, Barbara Fenton—maybe your history-professor-track-coach, for scratching his star sprinter."

"Very funny," Julie said. "Maybe it was suicide in remorse for killing Scooter."

"People don't commit suicide with ice picks," Lee Bidder informed her. "At least not when guns are handy. Didn't you hear Mike say there was a gun in the apartment?"

Pete pushed back his chair and got to his feet. "Let's go downstairs and ask Dinny Cord some more questions," he said to Linc and Julie.

Dinny Cord and Johnny Merlin were in separate

cells in the Felony Section. The cells there were clean and modern, but not very homey. The white porcelain fixtures and double-decker bunks, while antiseptically clean, were not exactly aesthetically appealing. Instead of bars, the front walls were of shatterproof herculite glass. The only bars were on the doors.

Pete, Linc and Julie stopped before the cell Cord was in and looked through the bars of the door. The prisoner was alone in the cell and was seated on the lower bunk.

Cord looked up and said in his high-pitched voice, "Morning."

"Morning," Pete said. "The police didn't find a knife on Eddie's body, Dinny. Or anywhere in his apartment."

"I been thinking about that," Cord said. "I may have it figured."

"All right. Let's hear it."

"When Eddie came to my place to tell me about you guys being cops, he also told me that young Scooter was roaring mad at somebody. Who, he didn't say, and I wasn't interested enough in the kid's problems to ask. But Eddie said the kid had borrowed the equipment from him to cut whoever he was mad at down to size. You think maybe he was talking about loaning the Miller kid his switchblade?"

The three members of the Mod Squad exchanged startled looks. Julie said, "But if Scooter had the knife, how did. . . ."

She let it trail off, and her eyes grew enormous.

Linc said to the man in the cell. "Eddie mention why Scooter was sore at this person? Was it the one who blew the whistle on him, for instance?"

Dinny Cord looked surprised. "If I had thought that, I'd have been more interested, because whoever blew the whistle on the kid, blew it on the rest of us, too. I really didn't pay too much attention to what Eddie said about it, because I didn't think it had anything to do with me, and I was too busy trying to work out my own problems."

Pete said, "Do you have any idea if the person Scooter was mad at was male or female?"

After considering, Cord said, "Now that you mention it, it must have been a woman. Eddie made another peculiar remark that didn't make much sense to me but which I didn't follow up, because I was too busy planning to lam into hiding. He said something to the effect that if his stupid niece got her face marked up, it would serve her right for being such a rat."

Pete, Linc and Julie looked at each other again. Linc said, "Are you guys thinking the same thing I am?"

Pete said, "I'm thinking that a female judo expert could take a knife away from a man without much trouble, even if she was only half his size. Let's go check Eddie Kye's package again, and see if any nieces are listed among his known relatives."

Ten minutes later, they were studying the dead man's record in the Golden Horseshoe. The information they wanted was on file, all right. All three of them must have skimmed over it previously without having its significance register.

Among Eddie Kye's known relatives was listed a widowed sister, who worked as a telephone operator in San Francisco. Her name was Mrs. Bernice Evans.

"I guess that does it," Pete said. "But why didn't Eve admit what had happened? If Scooter pulled that knife on her, meaning to cut her face in revenge for turning him in, it was self-defense on her part."

"But why her Uncle Eddie, too?" Linc asked. "That couldn't have been self-defense."

"Suppose we go ask her?" Pete suggested.

Eve Evans didn't have any Saturday classes, either, apparently. When the female clerk on desk duty at the girl's dorm rang the section where Eve lived, whoever answered the phone reported that the girl was in.

"Tell her she has visitors in the lobby," the clerk said.

A few minutes later Eve, in slacks and a sweater and thong sandals, came downstairs. She seemed surprised to find three people waiting for her. She looked from Julie to Linc to Pete inquiringly.

"You remember Julie Barnes, don't you, Eve?" Pete said. "She's the good friend who tipped you off about the bribery investigation."

The brunette flushed and said nothing. Pete glanced

at the female desk clerk, then took Eve's elbow and steered her toward the door.

"What we have to talk about is pretty private," Pete said pleasantly but firmly. "We'd better go outside."

Eve made no resistance.

CHAPTER 26

HOLDING her by the elbow, Pete propelled the girl through the door, across the driveway circling past the dormitory and onto the parking lot. Between the rows of cars, he released his grip and leaned against the front fender of an empty Nova. Linc and Julie halted, too, and examined Eve expressionlessly. The brunette nervously clasped her hands together and looked around the circle of faces.

"You kind of suspect what's coming, don't you, Eve?" Pete said.

The girl licked her lips. "I don't know what you mean," she said huskily.

"Sure you do." He took out his I.D. and held it for her to see. "This may be a surprise to you, though."

Eve's eyes widened as she examined the I.D. Looking up, she said with a tremor in her voice, "You're a cop!"

"Uh-huh," Pete said, replacing the I.D. in his pocket. "Linc and Julie, too. Now I have to warn you that you are not required to make a statement of any kind, and if you do, whatever you say may be taken down and used in evidence against you. Also, you are entitled to a lawyer, and if you can't afford one, you'll be furnished one at public expense if you ask for it."

The girl licked her lips again. "Are you arresting me?"

Pete nodded. "On suspicion of homicide."

Eve's eyes darted around the circle of faces. "How did you know?" she asked.

"We found out that the switchblade knife belonged to Eddie Kye, and that Scooter had borrowed it. Scooter never asked you to take him back, did he? He lured you to that bench because he planned to carve you up a little in revenge for ratting on him."

The girl's nervousness was suddenly and rather startlingly replaced by a blaze of anger. "I'm glad I killed him," she spat. "He said he loved me. He said that Fenton girl had been a mistake, and he never should have left me. I was in seventh heaven. I thought everything was going to be like it used to be. I was so happy, I could have burst. Then, after we got to that isolated spot, he suddenly began calling me names and raging that I had ruined his life. It was like Dr. Jekyll and Mr. Hyde. One minute he was all love and tenderness, the next he was a raving maniac. He yelled at me that he was going to be expelled, and maybe even go to prison, and I had done all that to him. I stood there stunned, hardly able to believe my ears. I couldn't even move until he flicked open that knife and said he was going to fix my face, so that no one would ever want me."

She stopped, almost panting with rage at the remembered scene.

"But then you moved?" Pete prompted gently.

"Of course. I took the knife away from him."

"How?"

Her anger at the dead boy was beginning to flow away again. Frowning at Pete, she said, "You mean you want me to show you?"

"Sure," he said. Straightening away from the fender he was leaning on, he took a ball-point pen from his pocket and thrust it toward the girl. "Pretend that's a knife."

Pete had a pretty good knowledge of judo himself, but the girl moved so fast that she caught him by surprise. Crossing her forearms, the right on top of the left, she grasped his right arm at the wrist and elbow. Simultaneously pushing down with her left hand and pulling upward with her right, she spun and knocked Pete off balance by sharply swinging her left hip against his right one.

He ended up flat on his face, his right arm twisted

up behind him and with her knee in the middle of his back. The pen tumbled from his nerveless fingers.

Eve picked up the pen and rose to her feet. Pete got up, brushed himself off and scowled at Linc, who looked as though he was maintaining a poker face with difficulty. Julie looked more bemused than amused.

Eve handed Pete back his pen, and he put it in his pocket.

He said, "You had him helpless, Eve. You could have picked up the knife and have heaved it off into the darkness, if you were afraid of him getting hold of it again. You didn't have to stick it in his back."

"No," she agreed unemotionally.

"It makes the difference between justifiable homicide in self-defense and at least manslaughter," he said carefully.

"I never thought of it as self-defense," she said in a contemptuous tone. "It nearly killed me inside when he turned on me like that, but I wasn't afraid of him physically. I knew I could handle Scooter, because he didn't know anything at all about judo, and I'm pretty good. But don't you understand? He lured me there under the pretense that he still loved me, then tried to ruin my looks."

Pete said, "I don't think you ought to talk anymore until you see a lawyer."

Linc said, "She couldn't cop a self-defense plea on the other one anyway, Pete. How about Uncle Eddie?"

Eve gave Linc a wide-eyed look. "You know Eddie was my uncle?"

"Uh-huh. Why'd you kill him?"

She made no effort whatever to deny having killed the man. In an indignant tone, she said, "He tried to blackmail me."

"Oh?" Linc said. "When was this?"

"Thursday morning. He heard about Scooter on the 5 A.M. news, although I don't know why he was up that early. He knew exactly what had happened, because he had lent Scooter that knife and knew what Scooter intended to do with it. His own niece, and he didn't even care that I was going to be cut up."

"It is a kind of new low," Pete agreed.

"Of course, he was sore because I had broken up his

lucrative racket by turning in Scooter and him. That was his excuse for blackmailing me, too. He said I owed it to him."

"When did he ask for this blackmail?" Pete inquired.

"Only a couple of hours after he heard about Scooter's death on the radio. As soon as the switchboard here opened at 7 A.M., he phoned me and threatened to go to the police, unless I paid him five thousand dollars."

All three members of the Mod Squad regarded her curiously. Pete said, "Where did he expect you to get money like that?"

"Oh, he knew I had it. I was beneficiary to a ten-thousand-dollar insurance policy my father had taken out in addition to the insurance he left Mom. Dad set it up as an educational fund. Uncle Eddie knew there was still over seven thousand left in the account and that I had full control over it. He said two thousand ought to take me through what college I have left to go, so he'd take the balance."

"Is it in a local bank?" Pete asked.

Eve shook her head. "In San Francisco. But I have a local checking account and have arranged to have funds transferred as I need them from the San Francisco bank here. He knew I could swing it, all right. He told me to bring him a postdated check, which would give me the necessary time to make arrangements with both banks. And he insisted on immediate payoff. He said he had already stuck around his apartment longer than was safe, and he wanted to get out of there. He gave me until 9 A.M. to get there, and said he would call the police if I hadn't showed up by then. I got there at a quarter to nine."

Linc said, "But you took along an ice pick instead of your checkbook, huh? Where'd you get it?"

"From the kitchen of the girls' dorm."

Linc glanced at Pete, who said, "I guess we've got enough. You want to pack something, Eve? Julie will go to your room with you, if you do."

"Are you taking me to jail?" the girl asked, looking around at all their faces.

"Afraid we have to," Pete said.

Up to now her still-smoldering anger at both her victims had not only sustained her, but had made her seem to be getting some kind of perverse satisfaction from recounting what she had done. But all of a sudden the realization of the enormous trouble she was in seemed to hit her.

She began to cry.

The following Monday morning, the Mod Squad met in Captain Greer's office for a staff conference.

The bribery investigation at Baldwin Hills College was being closed, the captain informed them. It was impossible to continue it without Dinny Cord's cooperation, and he refused to give it. The gambling ring was effectively broken up by the death of one of the ringleaders and the jailing of the other two on much more serious charges than bribery and conspiracy to defraud. But, all this really amounted to was that the athletes, aside from Scooter Miller, who had been accepting brides, would remain unkown.

"They lucked out," the captain concluded. "Instead of being expelled or even facing trial, they got away with it because a hood, who ordinarily wouldn't protect his own grandmother unless there was something in it for him, is afraid to talk."

"Dinny's still having nightmares about the Mafia, huh?" Linc said.

"I imagine that's what's keeping him silent. He and Merlin's hearings on the kidnapping and attempted murder charges are tomorrow, incidentally. You three will have to be in court at nine o'clock."

"We'll be there," Pete said.

Julie asked, "What's the D.A. doing about Eve Evans?"

"He's charging her only with the second murder. Scooter Miller's is too sticky. Even with her confession to you that she knifed him deliberately after she had him disarmed, the D.A. figures any good lawyer could get a self-defense verdict. He thinks it may be difficult to get more than a manslaughter verdict for the Kye murder, even. She's now claiming that she took the ice pick along in self-defense, because her uncle had struck her a couple of times in the past. She's also claiming that she used it only when he did attempt to hit her.

The jury may believe her, because juries aren't very sympathetic to blackmailers."

Pete said, "I really can't wish her any more than a manslaughter bust. Eddie Kye is no loss to society."

"Eve doesn't appear to be much nicer a person than her uncle, though," Captain Greer said. "She was the one who initially introduced Scooter to Eddie Kye, with the deliberate purpose of getting him involved in the bribery racket. She hasn't admitted it, but the D.A. suspects her uncle paid her to sell Scooter on the deal. Then, when Scooter jilted her, she ratted on him for doing something he never would have gotten involved in, if it hadn't been for her."

Linc said, "No wonder he was sore enough to want to carve her up a little."

"I still kind of feel sorry for her," Pete said a trifle wistfully.

Julie gave him a strange look. "Do you have some kind of romantic hang-up on the girl?" she inquired.

"Of course not," he said. "How's your romance coming, incidentally?"

She blushed slightly. "You mean Barney? He's taking me to dinner tonight."

"I've got a date tonight, too," Linc said. "Althea decided to forgive me for being a cop and being party to the arrest of her roommate. Why don't you get one, Pete, and make it a double?"

"I doubt that they'd let Eve out of jail," Pete said dryly.

"How about Barb Fenton? You seemed to like her. And she could probably stand the cheering up."

An interested expression appeared on Pete's face. "Yeah," he said. "I'd kind of like a chance to demonstrate that I wasn't being nice to her just because I wanted to pry information out of her, anyway. I'll give her a ring."

Captain Greer said, "In making all these social plans, just keep in mind that you have to be in court at 9 A.M. So you'd all better arrange to get in early."